Enid Blyton's
CHRISTMAS TALES

Look out for more enchanting story collections

from Enid Blyton . . .

The Brer Rabbit Collection
Cherry Tree Farm
Christmas Stories
Fireworks in Fairyland
Holiday Stories
Mr Galliano's Circus
Summer Stories
The Wizard's Umbrella

published by Hodder Children's Books

Enid Blyton's

CHRISTMAS TALES

Hodder
Children's
Books

First published in Great Britain in 2016 by Hodder Children's Books

A Catalogue record for this book is available from the British Library

ISBN 978 1 444 93113 6

Printed and bound in Great Britain by Clays Ltd, St Ives plc

MIX
Paper from
responsible sources
FSC® C104740

Hodder Children's Books
An imprint of Hachette Children's Books
Part of Hodder & Stoughton
50 Carmelite House,
Victoria Embankment,
London, EC4Y 0DZ
An Hachette UK company

www.hodderchildrens.co.uk

Contents

Introduction   vii

One Christmas Eve   1

All the Way to Santa Claus   13

Annabelle's Little Thimble   29

A Coat for the Snowman   39

The Extraordinary Christmas Tree   49

On His Way Home   59

The Golden Key   67

No Present for Benny   85

First Walk in December   93

The Christmas-Tree Fairy   111

A Christmas Legend   121

The Christmas Bicycle   129

A Grand Visitor   143

The Little Carol-Singer   157

The Man Who Wasn't Father Christmas   167

A Christmas Wish   179

He Belonged to the Family   191

A Hole in her Stocking   207

Christmas in the Toyshop   217

They Didn't Believe in Santa Claus!   241

Bobbo's Magic Stocking   253

The Pantomime Wolf   293

Little Mrs Millikin   307

Second Walk in December   321

The Magic Snow-Bird   337

Acknowledgements   355

Introduction

Enid Blyton loved Christmas. She enjoyed decorating her house (not just the Christmas tree), giving presents, sending and receiving cards (they covered every surface of her living room), and being with her family. She loved writing, of course, as well – she wrote over 600 books in her long career. So it's no wonder she combined the two and wrote many stories about Christmas. Here is a selection of them for you to enjoy.

These stories were written many years ago – some of them in the 1920s and 30s – so some of the details might seem unfamiliar to you. But they share what is still important about Christmas today – the spirit of giving, shared times, and lots of food and fun and family.

Happy reading! Happy Christmas!

One Christmas Eve

One Christmas Eve

ONE CHRISTMAS EVE something most extraordinary happened to Father Christmas. Two of his reindeer were new ones and didn't know one chimney from another – and suddenly his sleigh drew up beside a tall factory chimney!

Well, of course, it is no good going down a factory chimney, because there are never any children below with stockings to be filled. But Father Christmas was so used to his reindeer stopping at all the right chimneys that he didn't even look to see if this was a proper one.

'Out we get!' he said to himself, heaving at his

enormous sack. 'Stand still, reindeer, till I come back. My, what a pitch-dark night!'

He groped about for the chimney and found the rim. He lowered himself into it, and then, just as he usually did, he let himself go. He thought he would slip down the chimney a little way and then come to a fire-place.

Instead, he fell down and down and down at a most alarming speed! The chimney was very tall indeed, very black inside, and rather smelly. Father Christmas lost his red hat trimmed with white fur. His coat caught on a jutting nail, and was ripped off his back. It broke his fall, though, and when he at last landed at the bottom of the big factory chimney he only got a jolt and bump that made him gasp and sit down suddenly.

He felt himself all over. 'I'm not hurt. I've still got my sack. But I've lost my hat and my coat. Oh dear – I must look a dreadful sight, without a coat, and all black and sooty. How do I get out of here?

That must have been a factory chimney!'

He tried all the doors, but they were locked. So he opened a window and climbed out, pulling his sack behind him.

And then suddenly a loud voice hailed him and a bright lantern flashed its light in his sooty face.

'Hey, you there! What are you doing in that factory! And what have you got in that sack?'

It was a policeman! Father Christmas wasn't afraid of them because he had never in his life done anything wrong, and he liked them. But he really felt very awkward indeed at that moment, climbing out of a factory window.

'Er – it's all right, policeman,' he said. 'I'm – er – well, I'm Father Christmas, to tell you the truth.'

'That's a fine tale!' said the policeman in a disbelieving voice. 'Can't you think of a better one than that? Father Christmas indeed! You look more like a sweep! Open up that bag! I shall want you to give me the contents *and* come along to the police station with me!'

Father Christmas stared at him in horror. Give up his precious sack of toys – so that the children couldn't have any? Spend the night in prison? No, no, he couldn't possibly do that. He tried again.

'My good man, I'm telling the truth. I've had an accident and come down the wrong chimney – but I really *am* Father Christmas! Can't you see my reindeer up there?'

The policeman couldn't. He didn't even bother to look. He made a grab at Father Christmas and his sack!

Father Christmas ran for his life, and the policeman thundered behind him. Father Christmas came to a little gate, darted through it and hid behind a bush. The policeman missed the gate and went on – but Father Christmas knew he would soon be back! Whatever was he to do?

He went to the little house nearby, and peeped through a window. He saw two children in bed, with a little night-light shining beside them. He tapped at the window softly.

The children awoke. They sat up. Father Christmas tapped the pane again and called softly.

'It's me – Father Christmas. Let me in.'

The boy and the girl looked at one another in delight. Father Christmas! What a wonderful thing!

'He couldn't get down our chimney! I told you it was too small,' said the boy, and slid out of bed. 'I'll let him in.'

He opened the window wide and Father Christmas climbed in, shutting the window behind him. He was very glad to be out of the way of that angry policeman.

But the children didn't like the look of him at all. Where was his red hat and red coat? Why was he so black and dirty? They looked at him, scared.

'Ssh! Don't be frightened,' said Father Christmas. 'I came down the wrong chimney and lost my coat and hat and got dirty. Look – I'll open my sack, then you'll know I really *am* Father Christmas! All my toys are here!'

So they were! The sack was crammed absolutely full of toys of all kinds. The children gazed at them in the greatest delight.

'Poor Father Christmas,' said the girl, patting his arm. 'I'm sorry you came down the wrong chimney. Would you like a wash?'

The heavy tread of the policeman was heard outside. 'That's a policeman who thinks I'm a burglar,' said poor Father Christmas. 'Could you hide me, do you think – just till he goes?'

'Get into that cupboard,' said the boy. 'There's plenty of room for you. Quick! The policeman is knocking at the front door.'

So he was! Soon the children's parents were opening it in surprise, and listening to the policeman. 'The burglar may be hiding somewhere in your house,' he said. 'His footsteps go through your gateway! May I search, please?'

So he hunted all through the house – but he didn't look in the cupboard in the children's room, because the children's mother was quite, quite sure no one could get in there without being seen.

'The children would see a burglar if he got into their room and hid in the cupboard,' she said. 'They would call out in fright.'

The policeman gave up the hunt and went away. The children's parents went back to bed. And at last the cupboard door opened and Father Christmas looked out at the children, smiling.

'Thank you!' he said. 'I'll wash now. I only wish I could borrow a red hat and coat. I don't feel right without them!'

'Daddy's got one,' said the little girl. 'He went to a Christmas party – a fancy dress one – and he dressed up as Father Christmas. Borrow his coat and hat – they are just right, red, trimmed with white fur.'

Well, they fitted Father Christmas beautifully, and soon, washed and clean, and dressed up in proper

Christmassy clothes again, he was ready to go.

'Thank you very, very much for all your help,' he said to the two children. 'I don't know what I would have done without you. I'll go now.'

'Where are your reindeer?' asked the little girl.

'Somewhere up in the sky, wondering why I don't climb out of that factory chimney!' said Father Christmas. 'I'll whistle them down.'

He gave a peculiar whistle, and almost at once there came the sound of jingling bells, and down from the sky came the reindeer, drawing the sleigh behind them.

Father Christmas got in and set his big sack carefully down beside him. He spoke sternly to his reindeer.

'You two new ones aren't thinking what you are doing! Listen to what the older ones say, and don't stop at the wrong chimneys!'

He waved to the children. 'Goodbye! I shall have to hurry now or I'll never get finished before dawn.

Thank you again for your help. I'll send these clothes back as soon as I can.'

Off he went into the air, the reindeer galloping swiftly, their bells jingling as they went. The sound grew fainter and fainter – and then the children could hear it no longer. They went back to bed, excited.

'To think we were able to help old Father Christmas like that!' said the boy. 'What will the other children say when we tell them?'

'We'd better not say a word,' said the little girl. 'They just wouldn't believe us! I say – look – he's forgotten to fill *our* stockings!'

The two stared at their stockings, which they had hung at the ends of their beds. They hung limp and empty, with not a single toy. It was very, very disappointing.

'Well, I expect his adventure made him forget our stockings,' said the boy, at last. 'Never mind – we've shared in his adventure. Let's go to sleep.'

But, ah – what a surprise they are going to get in

the morning when they go to that cupboard that Father Christmas hid in! It's full of toys! A stockingful wasn't enough for those two kind children – Father Christmas wanted to leave them more than that!

And when they open that cupboard, out will come a train and a doll and a ship and a top and a book and a musical-box and a bear and a ... well, almost everything you can think of.

Wouldn't I love to be there when they open the door! Good old Father Christmas, I hope he always finds kind children to help him when he's in trouble!

All the Way
to Santa Claus

All the Way
to Santa Claus

THERE WAS a tremendous noise in the castle of Santa Claus. The workers there were getting thousands of toys ready for Christmas.

Tops were humming, toy ducks were quacking, rocking horses were rocking, trains were rattling round and round rails, and teddy bears were practising their growls. Everywhere you went you could see and hear the toys being made ready by the workers of Santa Claus.

Now one of the little workers was a brownie called

Slick. He was the one that taught the Jack-in-the-Boxes to jump straight out of their boxes on their springs, and make people jump. Nobody liked him very much. He didn't always tell the truth, and he was rather sly.

'I don't trust him,' said one brownie to another, as they worked hard with all the toys. 'Santa Claus ought to get rid of him.' But Slick was such a very good worker that Santa Claus didn't want to send him away.

This was a pity, because Slick had a very daring plan in his mind. He meant to steal the sack of toys that Santa Claus was going to take out with him on Christmas night!

This sack was a very magic one. It was a big one, of course, but it was magic, because although it looked as if it could hold about a hundred toys, actually it could hold as many as Santa Claus meant to give away on Christmas night!

Slick had found out all about this. He had asked

Mr Hessian, who always made each year's sack, how Santa Claus got the toys there. 'It's easy!' said Mr Hessian, busy sewing at the big sack. He sewed a bit of magic into every stitch. 'On Christmas night a whistle is blown, and all the toys stand up. Then they march out of their different toy-rooms in a long line, and walk straight into the sack. It doesn't matter how many there are, they can all go in. Then Santa Claus ties up the neck of the sack, and goes off with it in his sledge.'

That was all that Slick wanted to know. Now he knew what to do! 'I'll pretend that there is to be a *practice* march into the sack this year,' he said to himself. 'And *I'll* be the one to hold the sack open for the toys to march in! Then I'll tie up the sack, drag it to my car, and drive off with it into the Land of Boys and Girls. I'll sell the toys to all the toy shops and make a lot of money! How easy!'

So, some time before Christmas, Slick pretended to all the toys that there was to be a practice march into the sack. 'When I blow my whistle, you must all come,' he said.

He blew his whistle. At once the bears got up and marched growling to the sack. The ducks waddled and quacked. The trains rushed in at top speed and so did all the toy cars. The dolls walked in and the balls rolled along; the tops spun themselves there and even the bricks somehow hopped, skipped and jumped along. As for the toy soldiers, they marched smartly behind their captain who, with his sword drawn, saw them all carefully into the big sack.

It really was a sight to see.

'It's only a practice march,' whispered the dolls to one another. 'We shan't be in this smelly sack very long!'

But, to their great dismay, Slick tightly tied up the neck of the sack and began to drag it along the floor to the back door, where he had his car waiting! Nobody heard the cries of the toys. It really was very easy for Slick to steal them all.

In two minutes the big castle was quite silent, for not a toy was left. No growling, no clattering, no rocking, no quacking. The toys were all crowded together in the magic sack, hundreds and hundreds of them, being driven off to be sold in our land.

The captain of the soldiers soon guessed that something was wrong. He yelled out to Slick.

'Hi! What are you doing with us? Where are you taking us? Let us out! I shall complain to Santa Claus!'

Slick laughed loudly. 'You'll never see him again. You're going to toy shops for people to buy. You won't be put into children's stockings!'

The toys were scared and upset. They all began to talk at once and the tops hummed so loudly that it was difficult to hear what was being said.

'Silence!' said the captain of the toy soldiers, in a loud voice. 'I have a plan. Please listen, all of you.'

The toys became quiet. The captain spoke in a low voice. 'I am not going to be sold in a toy shop! I mean to go back to Santa Claus. I have a sharp sword, toys, and I am going to cut a hole in this sack. I and my soldiers will escape through this, and any of you that like to follow us can do so. We will lead you back to Santa Claus!'

He then out a large hole at the back of the sack.

He marched out with his soldiers, and they found themselves at the back of the car. It was not going very fast, because there was snow on the ground, and Slick was driving slowly in case he skidded. One by one the soldiers dropped to the snowy ground and all the toys followed them. Soon the sack was quite empty but Slick didn't know that. Oh, no, he drove on and on, thinking that he still had hundreds of toys behind him!

It was about six o'clock in the evening. They were in a big town, and they could see houses all round them. What should they do next?

'There's a policeman! Shall we ask him the way back to Santa Claus?' whispered a big doll.

So they made their way in a long line over the snow

to the big policeman. But when he saw this strange collection of tiny things moving towards him, he was afraid. He couldn't see that they were only toys, he thought they must be rats, and he ran off to the police station. 'Rat poison!' he said to himself. 'I must get some somewhere! What a plague of rats we've got in this town, to be sure!'

'He's run away,' said the captain, crossly. 'Look – here's somebody else – two people. Oh, they're children!'

Sure enough, two children were coming along in the snowy night. The soldiers followed their captain to a lamppost, and there the children saw them, a long line of little shining toys.

'Look, Betty – toy soldiers – and oh, my goodness, there are dolls too, hundreds of them. Are we dreaming?'

'We must be, Tom,' said Betty. 'But it's a lovely dream. Listen – this little soldier is speaking to us!'

'Do you know the way to Santa Claus?' the captain

was asking, in a little, high voice. 'Somebody stole us away from his castle tonight, and we want to go back.'

Well, of course, Betty and Tom made the same answer that *you* would have made. 'We don't know! We know he lives in a castle somewhere in a snowy land where reindeer live, but we couldn't possibly tell you the way!'

'Good gracious! But we really *must* get back!' said a big doll, in alarm. 'It's almost Christmas time and we're the toys that Santa Claus puts into children's stockings! We're not shop toys.'

'A reindeer could tell us the way,' said the captain. 'All reindeer know the way to the land of Santa Claus. You don't happen to have a pet reindeer we could ask, do you?'

'Oh, no!' said Betty, with a laugh. 'But there are reindeer at the London Zoo, and that's not very far away from here. This is London, you know.'

'Is it really?' said the captain, who had never in his life heard of London. 'Could you possibly take us to this Zoo, and let us talk to the reindeer?'

'It's shut now,' said Tom. 'But we could take you to the gates, and as you are so small you could easily slip through the railings. We'll take you to the gates that are nearest the reindeer house.'

'I don't know how to thank you,' said the captain. 'I shall certainly tell Santa Claus all about you when we get back, and I will ask him to bring you a special lot of toys this Christmas to reward you for your help.'

'What are your names?' asked the big doll, as they all walked down the street through the snow.

'I'm Tom and my sister is Betty,' said Tom. 'I say, this *is* a funny thing to happen! I do wonder if I'm dreaming it!'

After some time they came to the gates of the big London Zoo. It was quite easy for the toys to slip through the railings. They called goodbye and went into the dark grounds of the Zoo. They heard a wolf howling, and they heard owls hooting. And then they smelt the familiar smell of reindeer!

The captain sniffed hard. 'I smell them,' he said. 'Their house must be somewhere near here. Come along.'

So, through the Zoo, along the snowy paths, went a long, long line of toys, all behaving very well except one sailor doll who began to throw snowballs at the soldiers, and even threw one at a surprised bear who had wandered out into his open-air enclosure to see what the line of tiny creatures could be.

They came to the reindeer house at last and they all slipped through the railings. The reindeer were asleep. There were two of them, and the captain poked them with a sharp end of his sword. They woke up with a jump.

'Who's that?' said one reindeer.

'Reindeer, do you know Santa Claus?' asked the captain.

'Of course,' said the reindeer. 'I used to live not far from his castle. I always hoped I'd be chosen to draw his sledge, but I never was. I even practised galloping through the sky, you know, like his sledge reindeer do. But I wasn't fast enough.'

'Reindeer! Somebody stole all of us Christmas toys from the castle of Santa Claus,' said the captain earnestly. 'But we escaped. And now we want to get back. Could you possibly, possibly, tell us the way?'

'Well, you want to go the sky-way – it's much shorter than any other way,' said the reindeer. 'See that big star there? Well, you go straight for that, but at midnight you steer by those three stars to the right ... and ...'

The listening toys groaned. 'We can't fly through the sky!' said the big doll. 'Oh, reindeer, have you forgotten how to gallop through the air? Could you – could you *possibly* take us on your back, do you think? Think how grateful Santa Claus would be to you.'

The reindeer began to get excited. The second one did, too. They tried to remember the spell that had to be used for galloping in the sky over the big London Zoo, while the toys watched from below in delight!

One of the keepers saw the reindeer in the sky, but he didn't believe it. 'There's something wrong with my eyes,' he said. 'Reindeer in the sky, indeed! Why, I'll be believing in Santa Claus next!' So he didn't do anything about them at all, which was a very good thing.

It wasn't long before the toys were all climbing on to the reindeers' backs. They were not only on their backs, but on their necks and noses and tails and underneaths! There were so very many toys, you see. They all managed to get on at last and then – off they went! It was most exciting to gallop through the sky. There was no sound of hoofs, of course. The toys had to cling on tightly because the reindeer went so fast.

At last they arrived at the castle of Santa Claus, and the reindeer stamped up the steps puffing and blowing and feeling very important. And down the steps came Santa Claus and all his workers in the greatest surprise and delight.

'Why did you run away, toys? Where have you been?' cried Santa Claus. 'Who are these fine reindeer?'

The captain of the toys explained, and there was such an excited humming and quacking and squeaking and growling all around that Santa Claus could hardly hear.

'That wicked Slick!' he cried. 'I'll have him punished! And I'll reward both Betty and Tom, and these two reindeer as well. Reindeer, what reward would you like?'

'Oh, please, Santa Claus, may we help to draw your sledge on Christmas Eve?' begged the reindeer. 'We could gallop here from the Zoo.'

'Right!' said Santa Claus. 'Come along on Christmas Eve at about eight o'clock, so that I can get you ready. And now – what about these children, Betty and Tom? I'd better take them an extra fine lot of presents, I think. What is their address, captain?'

Well, will you believe it, nobody knew!

'I forgot to ask for it,' said the captain. 'And I don't know their surnames, either. Oh dear, how will you reward Betty and Tom now, Santa Claus?'

'I'll have to look up *all* the Bettys and the Toms in my Christmas book,' said Santa Claus, 'and I'll leave all of them some extra fine toys. That's the only thing I can do! Now come along to bed, each of you. You must be tired out.'

Well, that is the story of how all the Christmas toys were stolen, and how they got back safely to Santa Claus. I hope your name happens to be Betty or Tom. If it is, you'll be lucky this year.

Annabelle's
Little Thimble

Annabelle's
Little Thimble

ANNABELLE HAD a nice little work-basket that Granny had given her. You should have seen it! There were needles of all sizes, a bright pair of scissors, black, white, grey, green and blue cottons, and a pin-cushion. But best and brightest of all was Annabelle's little silver thimble.

Mummy had given it to her on her birthday. It was made of real silver, so it fitted Annabelle's middle finger beautifully, and she was very proud of it.

She took great care to keep her work-basket shut

when Rascal the Jackdaw was about. He was a tame jackdaw that Daddy had picked up from the ground when he was a tiny bird, fallen from the nest. Daddy had fed him and tamed him and now he hopped and flew around the house, and loved to talk to anyone he met.

But he was so fond of bright things that everyone was careful not to leave any spoons, brooches, necklaces or silver pencils about. If they did, Rascal the Jackdaw would take them and hide them away in one of his cubby-holes in the garden. Once Daddy had found a whole collection of things tucked away in a corner of the potting-shed – a pair of scissors, two spoons from next door, some pieces of silver paper and a little gilt pin!

Rascal couldn't help taking them because he was so fond of shiny things. Daddy had often smacked him on the beak for going off with things, but it didn't cure him! So everyone had to be very careful not to leave glittering things about.

Annabelle had always been careful of her little thimble, because she had seen Rascal looking at it two or three times, when she put it on her finger. But there came a morning when she forgot.

She was sewing a new bonnet for her doll when Mummy called her, 'Quick, Annabelle! There's Auntie Sue!'

Annabelle loved Auntie Sue so she hurriedly put down her work, stuck her thimble on top of it and ran to meet her auntie.

And as soon as she was safely out of the door Rascal the Jackdaw came in at the window! He spied the bright little thimble at once and pounced on it. Ah! He had wanted that for ever so long. Where should he put it?

He went and sat on the kitchen window-sill, holding it in his beak. Cook was busy making Christmas puddings, and she didn't even look at him. Rascal watched her. Dear me, Cook had lots of bright things too, on the table beside her!

Yes – she had six one pence pieces, four five pence pieces, a very small silver elephant, a tiny silver doll, a little silver horseshoe and one big, bright twenty pence. She was going to put them in the Christmas pudding for luck! It was always fun at Christmas time to see who got the treasures out of the pudding.

Rascal watched cook drop the shining things into the pudding. He thought Cook was hiding them. What a good place to hide them! He waited until Cook went to the cupboard to get something and then he hopped to the table. He dropped Annabelle's silver thimble into the sticky mixture and then covered it neatly up with the currants and chopped nuts in the dish. Ha! It was a splendid hiding place!

But oh dear me, what a to-do when Annabelle ran to get her sewing again! Where was her dear little silver thimble? Gone! Nowhere to be found at all! Everyone hunted all over the place, but it couldn't be found.

'Rascal must have taken it,' said poor Annabelle in

tears. So Daddy went to look in all the hidey-holes he knew the jackdaw had. But they were empty. Not one of them had Annabelle's thimble in it.

Annabelle was very unhappy. She did so like her thimble, and besides Mummy had given it to her. It was dreadful to lose something Mummy had bought for her. No other thimble would be half so nice!

'Perhaps someone will give you another one at Christmas time,' said Mummy, kissing her.

'It won't be as nice as the one *you* gave me, Mummy!' said Annabelle. 'It helped me sew so nicely. I shan't sew so well with any other thimble, I'm sure!'

'Rubbish!' said Mummy, smiling. She made up her mind to ask Annabelle's Auntie Sue to give the little girl another thimble for Christmas. Mummy wanted to give Annabelle a new doll. Auntie Sue promised Mummy she would buy a lovely new thimble for Annabelle.

But, you know, she forgot about it! Yes, she bought Annabelle a fairytale book instead – so when

Christmas came there was no silver thimble for Annabelle! She was so disappointed. But she didn't say anything, of course. She loved all her presents very much, especially her new doll – but she *would* have liked a new thimble!

Christmas dinnertime came. What a big turkey there was – and what a lot of people to eat it! Granny and Grandpa, three aunties, two uncles and Cousin Jane and Cousin Jimmy as well as Annabelle herself and Mummy and Daddy. But there was quite enough for everybody!

Then Cook brought in the Christmas pudding with a bit of holly stuck on top. How the children clapped their hands! What a splendid pudding it looked!

'Hope I get a five pence!' cried Cousin Jane.

'Hope I get a twenty pence!' cried Cousin Jimmy.

'And I hope I get the little silver elephant!' cried Annabelle. Everyone was served, and then what a hunt there was through the pieces of pudding to see if anyone had been lucky.

'A five pence for me!' cried Daddy. 'Hurrah!'

'Twenty pence for me!' cried Cousin Jimmy, fishing out a twenty pence from his piece of pudding.

'What have *I* got?' cried Annabelle, feeling her spoon scrape against something hard. She looked at the treasure *she* had and then she cried out in astonishment.

'Mummy! Daddy! It's my own little silver thimble that I lost ages ago! Oh, look! How did it come in the pudding?'

Mummy and Daddy *were* surprised! Annabelle ran out to ask Cook if she knew it had been put in the pudding, but Cook didn't know anything about it at all!

'I expect it's a little trick Santa Claus played on you!' she said.

'Caw, caw, caw!' suddenly said a loud voice, and Rascal the Jackdaw looked in at the window.

'Oh, Rascal, I wonder if *you* took my thimble and dropped it into the pudding!' cried Annabelle. 'Did you, Rascal?'

'Caw, caw, caw!' said the jackdaw. And Annabelle didn't know whether he meant yes or no! But she didn't mind; she had got back her little silver thimble after all. It was the nicest Christmas surprise she had had!

A Coat for
the Snowman

A Coat for
the Snowman

OLD MRS WHITE looked out of her bedroom window
and frowned. 'Snow!' she said. 'Snow – thick and white
and deep! How annoying. What a lot must have fallen
in the night.'

'Oh, look at the lovely snow!' shouted the children
in the field nearby. 'It's as high as our knees. Let's
build a snowman.'

'Silly children to play with the cold snow like that,'
said Mrs White, who wasn't very fond of children.
'Now I suppose they will play in the field all day and

make a terrible noise. Bother them all.'

Micky, Katie, Olivia, Peter and Will played together in the snowy field that day and had a lovely time. They made their snowman. He was a real beauty.

He had a big round head, with twigs sticking out for hair. He had eyes of stones and a big white stone for a nose. He had a stone mouth, too.

He had a big fat body, and the children patted it all round to make it smooth. He looked very real.

'We must dress him,' said Micky. 'We want a hat for him.' He found an old hat in a ditch. It just fitted the snowman nicely. He wore it a little to one side and looked very knowing indeed.

'We want a scarf, too,' said Katie. 'My aunt lives in that cottage nearby. I'll see if she has one.'

She had. It was an old red one, rather holey, but it went round the snowman's neck quite well.

'He'll feel warm with this scarf,' said Olivia. 'It must be so cold to be made of snow. I do wish we had a coat for him to wear.'

'Oooh yes – then we could fill the sleeves with snow and that would make him look awfully real,' said Katie. 'I'll ask my aunt for an old coat.'

But her aunt said no, she hadn't a coat old enough for a snowman.

'Where can we get one?' asked Katie. 'Shall I ask the old lady next door to you? What's her name? Mrs White?'

'Oh, you won't get anything out of her,' said her aunt. 'She doesn't like children. She's a grumbly old thing. You leave her alone.'

'She looks very poor,' said Olivia. 'Hasn't she got much money?'

'Hardly any,' said Katie's aunt. 'Don't you go bothering her, now – she'll box your ears if you do.'

The children went back to their snowman. They looked at him. It would be so very, very nice if he had a coat. He would be the finest snowman in the world then.

Just then old Mrs White, in big rubber boots, came

grumbling out to get herself a scuttleful of coal. Micky saw her.

'Poor old thing,' he said. 'I'll get the coal for her.' He hopped over the fence and went down the snowy garden. Old Mrs White saw him and frowned.

'Now, what are you doing coming into my garden without asking?' she scolded.

'I'll get your coal in for you,' said Micky. 'Give me that shovel.'

He shovelled until the scuttle was full. Then he carried it indoors for Mrs White.

'That's kind of you,' she said. 'But I hope you're not expecting money for that. I've none to spare.'

'Oh no, of course not,' said Micky, quite shocked. 'My mother won't let me take money for helping people. She says you are not really helping if you're paid. I don't want any reward at all, thank you, Mrs White.'

'Well now, I wish I could give you something, that I do,' said Mrs White, feeling pleased with the little boy. 'But I've no biscuits and no sweets. You just look round my kitchen and tell me if there's anything you'd like. What about that little china dog?'

'I don't want anything, thank you,' said Micky, looking round. He suddenly saw an old, old coat hanging up behind the kitchen door.

'Well,' he said, 'there's just one thing – do you think you could possibly lend us that old coat for our snowman, Mrs White? Only just *lend* it to us. We'll bring it back safely.'

'Why, yes, if you want it,' said old Mrs White. 'It's a dirty, ragged old thing. I haven't worn it for years. I keep meaning to give it away. Yes, you take it. I shan't even want it back.'

'Oh, thank you,' said Micky. 'Our snowman will look wonderful.'

He unhooked the old coat from the door and ran back to the others with it. 'Look what I've got!' he called. 'Mrs White's given it to me for our snowman. Won't he look great?'

The children filled the sleeves with snow and then hung the coat round the snowman. He certainly did look real now. There he stood in his old hat, scarf and coat, looking very smart.

'How do you do, Mr Shivers?' said Micky, walking up to the snowman and holding out his hand. 'I hope you like this cold weather.'

The others roared with laughter. The people passing by looked over the hedge at the snowman and called out that he was the best one they had seen. The children really felt very proud of him.

They left him standing there alone when it grew dark. But the next day they were back again. Alas, the snow had begun to melt, and Mr Shivers was a peculiar sight. He had slumped down, and all the snow had trickled out of his sleeves.

'He's going,' said Micky. 'I'll take Katie's aunt's old scarf back to her.'

'We don't need to take Mrs White's coat back. She said we could keep it,' said Peter. 'Still, perhaps we'd better.'

Micky jerked the coat off the melting snowman. He ripped the lining a little and some paper fell out.

'I say, what's this?' said Micky in surprise. 'Why, it's money. There's fifty pounds! It must have slipped out of the pocket into the lining, and old Mrs White didn't know it was there. Gracious, let's go and give it to her.'

They all tore off to Mrs White's cottage. She could hardly believe her eyes when she saw the money. 'Why, now, I lost that money years and years ago,' she said. 'And proper upset I was about it, too. Thought I'd dropped it in the street, and all the time it was in my coat-lining. What a bit of good luck for me.'

'Yes,' said Katie. 'I'm so glad.'

'Bless your heart! What nice children you are. Maybe I've been wrong about boys and girls,' said old Mrs White. 'Well, well, now I can buy myself a new cardigan and a new pair of shoes for my poor old feet.'

She bought something else, too. She bought the

biggest chocolate cake she could buy; she bought crisps and biscuits, a pound of mixed chocolates, five big balloons and a big box of crackers. And she gave a party for Micky, Katie, Olivia, Peter and Will.

They loved it. But in the middle of it Micky gave her quite a shock. 'There's somebody who ought to have come to this party and isn't here,' he said solemnly. 'What a pity.'

'Oh dear me, who's that?' said Mrs White, quite alarmed. 'I am sorry I've forgotten one of you. Go and fetch him at once.'

'We can't,' said Micky, and he laughed. 'It's Mr Shivers, the snowman, Mrs White. He ought to be the guest of honour, for without him we'd never have borrowed your coat and we wouldn't have found the money. What a pity old Mr Shivers isn't here.'

The Extraordinary
Christmas Tree

The Extraordinary
Christmas Tree

PING CAME racing into the kitchen, and startled his
brother Pong very much.

'Pong! 1 know where some magic Christmas trees
are growing. You know – the kind that flowers into all
kinds of lovely presents on Christmas Day! Shall we
take one tonight?'

'We shouldn't,' said Pong. 'But all the same – let's
do it! I'd love a magic Christmas tree that would grow
presents for us on every branch!'

So that night the two bad imps stole through the

darkness to where the magic Christmas trees grew in Witch Green-Eyes' garden. They climbed the wall, and slipped down the other side.

Ping had a spade. Pong had a sack. Ping dug up a nice little tree and Pong put it into his sack. Then they climbed back over the wall and ran at top speed to their cottage.

They hid it in the larder, in case anyone saw it. But on Christmas Eve they put it by the fire to warm the magic in it, and make it begin to bud and grow presents for them for the next day. The tree shook its green branches, and the two imps looked hard to see if any buds were growing.

But they couldn't see any. They went to bed and fell asleep, longing for Christmas Day to come. Santa Claus didn't go near their cottage. He knew quite well that they were bad imps, and he certainly wasn't going to leave them anything in their stockings.

In the middle of the night, Ping woke up. He heard a noise, a kind of windy sound in the kitchen.

What could it be?

He got out of bed and went to look. The kitchen was full of the sound of the wind, and the Christmas tree's branches were waving wildly. To Ping's surprise, the tree seemed to be about twice the size it had been!

'Pong!' he called up the stairs. 'Come and look at our tree. It has grown tremendously. But there aren't any presents budding on it yet!'

'Oh, go back to bed!' called Pong, sleepily. 'If it grows a bit, all the better for us! There will be more room on it for presents!'

So Ping went back to bed and fell asleep again. But early in the morning he was awakened by somebody making a noise on the bedroom floor. At least, that is what it sounded like! He leaned over the edge of the bed to see what it was – and dear me, what a shock he got!

The Christmas tree in the kitchen below was growing through the floor of the bedroom! It had gone right through the kitchen ceiling and was now waving its spiky topmost branch through a hole in the bedroom floor!

'Pong!' cried Ping in alarm. 'Quick! Look at the tree! It's grown much too large. We must stop it.'

But they couldn't, of course. Instead of taking a magic Christmas tree that grew presents, they had taken one whose magic made it grow enormous, and which could be used for a very big children's party. Witch Green-Eyes sold plenty of those. They didn't grow any presents at all.

Well, Christmas Day was a terrible day for Ping and Pong that year! The tree grew slowly up through the bedroom floor, taking the chest-of-drawers with it and upsetting the washstand. It grew right up to the bedroom ceiling.

And then it grew through that, and soon its topmost spike stuck out of the roof beside the chimney-pot. And all the little folk of the village came to stare in surprise.

Ping was crying. 'Go and fetch Witch Green-Eyes!'

he called to the villagers. 'Tell her to get her horrible tree!'

Witch Green-Eyes came to see it. She stood and laughed, and her black cat laughed with her.

'Well, well – it's a fine punishment for two dishonest little thieves!' she said. 'I don't want the tree back. You can keep it. I've no doubt it will stop growing soon – when it's taken the roof off your cottage!'

'Please, dear witch, please take it away,' begged Pong. 'We'll do anything you like if only you'll take it away.'

Witch Green-Eyes looked at him sharply. 'I'll take it away if you'll come and dig over the ground in my garden, once all the trees have been sold,' she said. 'It's hard work – but hard work will do you two good.'

'We'll come and do the digging. And we'll plant the magic seeds for next year's trees,' said Ping.

'Oh, no, you won't,' said Witch Green-Eyes. 'I'll do

that myself. It's easy. You can do all the digging, and that will save me a lot of trouble. Well – I'll take away this tree now.'

So she called out a string of magic words, and hey presto! The tree began to shrink back to its original size, a small tree no higher than Ping or Pong and carried on shrinking. Then the witch fetched it from the kitchen, and she and her cat stalked off, laughing loudly.

As for Ping and Pong, they had to mend their ceilings and roof, because the holes let in the snow and rain, and they didn't like that at all. They were very miserable indeed.

But they cheered up a bit when they got an invitation to a party in the village hall. They put on their best things and went off arm in arm.

But, oh dear, when they got to the hall, what did they see but the very Christmas tree, again grown enormously high, that they had stolen a few nights before, standing at the end of the hall. And when it saw the bad imps, the tree began to wave its big branches and make such a furious windy noise that the imps were scared and rushed out of the hall at top speed. So they didn't get a present off the tree after all. And now they have got to go digging in Witch Green-Eyes' garden – but nobody feels a bit sorry for them. Neither do I!

On His Way Home

On His Way Home

'THAT'S ALL for tonight,' said the choir-master. 'Richard, you sang better than ever. You've got more music in you than all the others here put together! I wish you could give them a little!'

Richard didn't even hear what the choir-master said. He was dreaming as usual, thinking out the tunes *he* could put to some of the carols they had been practising for Christmas week.

'Richard's dreaming of the time when he's grown-up and sings at concerts all over the world and makes more money than he'll know what to do with!' said one of the boys, who was jealous of Richard.

The choir-master looked at the dreamy Richard. He was certain that the boy would become famous when he grew up. He lived for his music and his singing, and what was more, he worked hard at it too.

'Yes,' he said, 'Richard will be richer than any of us. He won't be able to help it. But let's hope he'll think of others besides himself when success and wealth come to him!'

Richard was the last to go home. He always was because he was slow and didn't think what he was doing. But at last he went out of the church, and looked up into the frosty sky, full of stars.

As he turned a corner, he heard the sound of a violin, and he stopped. It was a cheap violin – but how beautifully it was being played. The player spoilt it, though, by trying to sing to the melody.

Richard looked at him. He was an old and dirty fellow, with straggly grey hair, and stained, ragged clothes. His voice was hoarse and cracked as he tried to sing the lovely old carols. People laughed at him.

Two boys sent a stone skimming down the road at him. No one threw money in the shabby hat put down at the man's feet.

'What a horrible noise!' said people passing by. 'We would give him money to go away, but none for his dreadful singing!'

Richard was struck by the man's playing. A poor, cheap violin – but how marvellously played. He went up to the man.

'I like the way you play,' he said. 'You play wonderfully!'

The old man took his bow from the strings and peered at the boy. 'I once had a famous name,' he said. 'I played all over Europe. Now I'm a poor old beggarman scraping a cheap violin – and I can't earn anything for a meal, nothing for a bit of fire, or a warm coat. But it's done me good to have a boy come and tell me I can still play! Can you play too?'

'I can sing,' said Richard. 'I'll sing to your violin, if you like. Play the tunes of the old carols and I'll sing for you. Perhaps you'll get some money if I sing and you play.'

The old man put his violin under his chin again. The first few notes of 'Silent Night' came stealing on the night-air.

Richard lifted his head. 'Silent night, Holy night,' he sang, his voice as pure as an angel's.

The old man stared in amazement and delight – what a voice! Ah, this boy was a pleasure to play for. Violin and voice mingled, and people passing by stopped suddenly. Who was this singing? Who was it playing? Two masters of music, surely! But under the light of the lamppost they saw only a young boy and an old and dirty beggar.

A little crowd gathered round, listening in silence. The choir-master came by on his way home, astonished by the voice, unable to believe it could be Richard's. The carol came to an end. A stream of coins poured into the hat. Richard looked down at the old hat in delight. What a lot of money!

The beggar ran his bow gently over the strings again. 'Noel! Noel!' sang the strings, and Richard's voice joined in, clear and lovely to hear in the dark, frosty night.

The crowd joined in at the end of each verse, and once more the money rained down into the old hat. Then a policeman loomed up apologetically.

'Sorry – but you must move on,' he said. The crowd sighed. What a pity! They had never heard carols they enjoyed more. Richard picked up the heavy hat and gave it to the old man.

'There must be enough here to buy you all you want this Christmas week!' he said. 'I'm glad.'

'Take half,' said the beggar, but Richard pushed the hat away.

'No. I couldn't take money for singing to your lovely playing. You have it all.' The boy ran home, humming a carol tune under his breath. The old man looked after him and the choir-master heard him muttering to himself.

'Ah, you'll be a great musician one day, my boy – and you'll be a great man too! You won't only think of your music – you'll think of your fellow-men.' And off went the old man with his pockets full of money – the first money that Richard had ever earned.

Good luck to you, Richard. You've begun the right way.

The Golden Key

The Golden Key

I DON'T know whether you noticed it, but one Christmas time not very many years ago your stocking was full of *little* things, and you had hardly any *big* presents at all. Thimbles, chocolate, soldiers, pencils, balls, and things like that, you had – no dolls' houses or forts, tricycles or big dolls. You may have wondered why. Well, there is usually a reason for everything, and there was certainly a reason for *that*.

It all happened really, because Santa Claus was careless one day in August.

He was visiting the country of the Nobbley Gnome to see if the Gnome had brought back any good ideas for new toys when he returned from his travels in strange lands. The Gnome was a great traveller, and used to go off every year by himself, taking about a hundred sacks with him, to collect all sorts of curios and old books. It sometimes happened that he came across a pretty or clever old toy, and as he knew Santa Claus was always willing to buy them from him, he used to bring them back in one of his sacks. He used little white donkeys to carry his sacks, and a very strange procession they made, wending over the country in a long laden line, with the Nobbley Gnome riding at the head.

In August he came back and sent a message to Santa Claus.

'I have some quaint toys for you,' said the message. 'Please come and see.'

'Good,' said Santa Claus, and rang a bell.

'Get my reindeer ready for me,' he said to the small elf who came running in. 'I am going to visit the Nobbley Gnome.'

Ten minutes later Santa Claus started off, and in the early evening he drew up at the Nobbley Gnome's little crooked castle on the top of Whistling Hill.

'Welcome!' called the Nobbley Gnome, opening his door and bowing low.

'Good evening,' said Santa, 'what a warm day it has been!' And he went into the castle.

Soon the Gnome was showing him a dolls' house in which lived two dolls, who walked about, and climbed the stairs, and went to bed.

'They go by clockwork,' said the Gnome, and he set them going for Santa Claus to see.

Then he showed him a book which could turn its own pages, and a collection of farmyard animals which could moo, or bleat, or crow, and a doll who could brush her own hair.

'These are quite clever,' said Santa Claus, 'but I'm not sure if I like them enough to buy them. Is there anything else?'

The Nobbley Gnome nodded.

'Yes,' he said, 'there's one thing more. Look!' and he put on the table a doll dressed just like a fairy, with long dainty wings.

'What can she do?' asked Santa.

'If I wind her up she can fly,' answered the Gnome. He took a small golden key out of his pocket, and fitted it into the doll's back.

Click, clicka-click! Click-clicka-click!

Suddenly the doll's wings moved, and she rose quietly and gracefully into the air, making a soft humming sound like a bee's. She circled round the room, and came to rest on the Nobbley Gnome's hands.

'Beautiful!' cried Santa, picking up the golden key to wind her up again. Then he looked closely at the key, and felt in his pocket.

'Why!' he said, bringing out another golden key very like the doll's key. 'Why, they're nearly alike, I declare! This is the key that locks up the door of the cave where I keep my magic Christmas sack!'

The Nobbley Gnome pricked up his large pointed

ears. He had often wondered about Santa's sack.

'It is a marvellous sack,' he said.

'It is,' said Santa, heartily. 'It's magic, of course. Otherwise I couldn't pack all the toys into it that I do. Do you know you could put as many things into it as you like, and it would never be really full.'

The Nobbley Gnome thought of all the many sacks he had to drag about with him when he returned from his travels, and he wished he had one like Santa Claus. Then an idea came to him.

'Do you want this wonderful doll?' he asked.

'Yes, rather!' answered Santa, taking out his fat purse. 'How much do you want for it?'

'I don't want money,' said the Gnome, 'I want that sack of yours. It would be so useful to me!'

'I daresay!' laughed Santa. 'But what would *I* do without it? I don't suppose there's another like it in the world.'

'Well, you can't have the doll, then,' said the Gnome sulkily.

'All right!' said Santa, putting away his purse and picking up the little golden key to put in his pocket. 'You shouldn't ask for impossible things, Sir Nobbley Gnome.'

He strode out of the castle, whipped up his reindeer, and drove away to Toyland again. He knew he had plenty of nice things for Christmas, so he didn't bother about the ones the Nobbley Gnome had. But what he *didn't* know was that he had carelessly picked up the *wrong* golden key, and put it in his pocket. He had left behind him the precoius key that locked up his magic sack, and in its place had pocketed the golden key which belonged to the fairy doll!

Now it happened that exactly a week before, Christmas Santa decided he had better get his magic sack and give it to Pixie Nimblefingers, to see if there were any holes in it.

So he left Toyland Castle, slipping out of the back door when no one was looking, and went down the hill to where Ivy Cave was. Very few folk knew what was kept there, for Santa Claus knew there were many bold goblins and dwarfs who would be glad to steal his wonderful sack if only they knew where it was.

Santa stopped when he came to a big curtain of ivy overhanging part of the cliff. He lifted it to one side, and there, behind it, was a small green door with PRIVATE marked on it.

Then he began looking for his golden key in all his pockets.

'Now where did I put it? Trousers pocket? No. Coat pocket? No. Waistcoat pocket? No. Ah – wait a minute. Yes! Here it is!' and he pulled out a little golden key. He slipped it into the lock, and tried to turn it.

But to his immense astonishment it wouldn't turn! Try as he would, the key didn't properly fit, and he couldn't unlock the door.

'Well!' said Santa Claus, taking out the key, and looking at it. 'Well! For hundreds of years you've unlocked that door, little key, and now you won't!'

He went back to the Castle, and called his servants.

'Bring axes!' he ordered. 'I want a door broken open.'

The servants trooped down the hills, carrying axes, and stopped at the cave.

Crash! Bang! Splinter!

The door was chopped down, and Santa stepped into the cave.

But the sack wasn't there!

Santa Claus stared in puzzled amazement.

'Where is my sack?' he cried at last. 'Here's a week before Christmas, and my sack has gone! Whatever shall I do?'

He couldn't make it out at all. It was all so puzzling. He had the key – but it wouldn't unlock the door – and the sack was gone!

'Has anyone strange been seen about here lately?' he asked sternly.

'No, Excellency,' replied his servants.

But suddenly a little voice piped out:

'I saw someone strange, Excellency!'

Santa looked down at a little sprite, standing on a toadstool to make himself taller.

'Who?'

'It was two months ago,' said the sprite, 'and I was sleeping one night in a blackbird's old nest hidden in the ivy. Suddenly someone swung the ivy back and unlocked that door. I peeped out, and it was a *very* ugly gnome, all bony and thin!'

'The Nobbley Gnome!' exclaimed Santa. 'I took the wrong key when I left his castle last August: I took the doll's key! O, dear me! How can I get my sack back in time?'

He went back to the cstle and called a meeting of all the chief fairies, elves, brownies, and pixies.

'What can we do about it?' he asked sadly.

'It is almost impossible to get it back in time,' said Queen Titania; 'and I doubt very much if the Nobbley Gnome would give it back, even if we asked him.'

Then Oberon spoke.

'You must use ordinary sacks, Santa,' he said, 'and

you must hurry up and get them. You'll need hundreds and hundreds. If I were you, I would take the children presents which are very tiny this year. Then you can get more into the sacks.'

'And I will go and see if I can make the thief give up the magic sack!' cried Pippit, the chief Pixie. 'But, in case I can't, have other sacks ready, for it will be hard to be successful.'

Off he went. And whilst he was gone, Santa began to be very busy. He ordered the Brownies to make big sacks as fast as ever they could. He told the Dwarfs to make him more sledges on which to carry the sacks, and he ordered more reindeer from the Land of the Frozen Giants. And he sent word all round Fairyland that he wanted the *smallest* gifts for boys and girls that Christmas. Anything big would have to wait for the following year.

Meanwhile, Pippit flew off to the Nobbley Gnome's house, and knocked on the front door. Tock, the gnome's servant, answered him.

'Where's your master?' demanded Pippit.

'Gone off travelling,' answered Tock.

'Oh dear!' sighed Pippit, in dismay. 'Has he taken all the donkeys, as usual?'

'No,' said Tock. 'Only two donkeys. One for himself and one for his sack. He's only taken one sack this time!'

'Yes, that's our sack!' thought Pippit angrily. 'Where's he gone to?' he asked aloud.

'To the Toadstool Country,' answered Tock. 'Away to the West.'

Pippit thought hard for a minute. 'I've got something to carry,' he said. 'Could you lend me one of your master's sacks?'

Tock pointed to a shed. 'There's hundreds in there!' he said. 'Take any you like.'

Pippit chose a brown one, as nearly like Santa's magic sack as he could find. He put it over his shoulder, and flew off to the Country of Toadstools.

It took him two days of hard flying to get there, but

at last, in the distance, he saw the huge toadstools which gave the country its name.

In each toadstool lived a quaint little elf, and Pippit knocked on the door of the first toadstool he saw.

'Has the Nobbley Gnome been here?' he asked.

'Yes,' answered the elf, 'he is wandering through the country, buying odd things from the Toadstool folk.'

'Thank you,' said Pippit, and flew off, with a great idea in his head. He soon found out exactly where the Nobbley Gnome was. He flew on ahead of him, and came to an empty toadstool. He found the elf who owned it, and got his permission to stay there for a night or two.

Then he hid his sack in a corner, and looked out for the Nobbley Gnome. Directly he saw hin, he hung out a notice on the toadstool:

BED and BREAKFAST CHEAP.

The Gnome, tired out, and longing for a night's rest, caught sight of the notice.

'How much do you charge?' he called to Pippit.

'Two cups of honey!' answered Pippit.

Now, the Nobbley Gnome thought that was remarkably cheap, and he at once tied up his two donkeys, and entered Pippit's toadstool.

Pippit gave him a good supper, and showed him a soft, downy bed. The Gnome lay down and fell fast asleep at once, with his half-full sack beside him.

Pippit ran outside, filled his own sack with wood and stones, and put it quietly down by the Nobbley Gnome's bed. Then he took the magic sack and started off with it through the dark night. He didn't dare to take one of the donkeys, for he was terrified that the Gnome would hear any noise he made and came after him.

The sack was very heavy, and Pippit couldn't fly with it; he could only walk slowly. He didn't know the magic which emptied the sack, and he was dreadfully afraid he would arrive at Toyland long after Santa had started off.

Nobody really expected Pippit to come back in time, and when Christmas Eve came everything was ready for Santa to start out. Scores of reindeer were harnessed to pull scores of sledges, and hundreds of sacks were placed on them, full of little tiny presents.

'I'll make a terrible clitter-clatter going through the streets!' sighed Santa. 'All the children will wake up and peep! Dear me! It's time to start!'

'Wait a little longer,' begged Titania, who had great faith in Pippit. 'Wait till the clock chimes midnight.'

'Very well,' said Santa. 'That will just give me time to drink another glass of hot cocoa. Brrrr-rrr! It's cold!'

Ding-dong-ding-dong! The Castle clock began to chime midnight, and Santa went out to get in his sleigh.

But hark! What was that?

'Stop! Stop! Stop!' called a faint voice. 'There's the magic sack!'

And Pippit staggered up the hill to the Castle, and put the sack at Santa's feet.

How everyone cheered him!

'Quick! said Santa. 'Empty all those scores of sacks out into the magic sack! There's no time to get other presents, so the children will have to put up with tiny ones. But I can at least take them in my magic sack!'

Quick as thought, all the sacks were emptied one by one into the marvellous magic sack. Thimbles, chocolates, soldiers, balls, pencils, and pens, all went tumbling in, and yet the sack was never full!

'Off we go!' shouted Santa Claus, merrily cracking his big whip over his reindeer's antlers – and off they galloped to our world at exactly twenty minutes past midnight! And before any child was awake on Christmas morning Santa had filled every stocking with the small presents tucked away in his bag – and now you know the reason why you had such little things in your stockings a few years ago.

As for Nobbley Gnome, just imagine his surprise when he found his sack full of wood and stones! He knew what had happened at once, and he was so afraid of what Santa Claus and the fairies would do to him if he ever went anywhere near Fairyland again, that he wandered right away to the Land of Deep Regrets and no one has ever heard of him since!

No Present for Benny

No Present for Benny

AMANDA WAS very happy. It was Christmas Day and she had had a lovely lot of presents. There had been plenty in her stocking, and some more on the breakfast-table. She had had just the things she wanted – a big new baby doll, a fine lot of books, and a new pencil-box full of lovely pencils.

And now they were all getting ready to go to Granny's for Christmas Day dinner. There would be an enormous turkey and a plum-pudding too. Grandpa would carve the turkey and make jokes. Auntie Susan would be there, and she was nice, too.

'There will be six of us at Granny's, won't there?'

said Amanda, counting.

'No, eight,' said Mummy. 'Auntie Lucy and her little boy, Benny, will be there, too. You remember him, don't you, Amanda? A dear little shy boy.'

'Oh, yes. I loved him,' said Amanda, thinking of the merry little boy, shy and kind, that she had played with at Auntie Lucy's the summer before. 'But oh, Mummy – I've just thought of something dreadful!'

'What?' said her mother, buttoning up Amanda's coat.

'I didn't know Benny was coming – so I haven't got a present for him,' said Amanda. 'Whatever shall I do?'

'It doesn't matter,' said Mummy. 'He won't mind. Come along now, we mustn't wait another minute or we shall miss the bus.'

Amanda hurried along the road, worrying about having no present for Benny. She liked giving everybody presents. She didn't like missing anyone out. She hadn't known Benny was going, or she would certainly have bought him a present. But now she had spent all her money and she couldn't even buy him one when the shops were open.

Benny was at Granny's, shy and smiling. He ran to Amanda and gave her a hug. And then he held out a parcel to her. 'Happy Christmas!' he said. 'I've brought a present for you.'

'Oh, Benny!' said Amanda, and felt worse than ever. She undid the parcel. Inside was a jigsaw puzzle, just the kind she liked. 'Thank you,' she said. 'You really are kind.'

She did wish she had a present for Benny. She thought he looked hurt because she didn't give him one. Amanda worried so much about it that it began to spoil her Christmas Day. Still, it didn't spoil her appetite for her dinner!

The turkey was carved by Grandpa, who made his usual funny jokes. Then came the Christmas pudding. It was a beauty, black as could be.

'I made it myself,' said Granny. 'I hope it will taste good.'

It did. It tasted lovely. But suddenly Amanda felt her teeth biting on something rather hard. She was puzzled. She took the hard thing out of her mouth and looked at it. It was an old sixpenny piece! 'Gosh, look what I've found in my pudding!' she said to Granny.

Granny laughed. 'Oh yes – I forgot to remind you all that there are old sixpenny pieces in the pudding. Now, Benny – perhaps you will find one too!'

But Benny didn't. He was very disappointed, because he knew Christmas pudding sixpences were special, lucky ones. And Amanda suddenly bit on something hard again in her very last mouthful – and there was another sixpence!

'You *are* a lucky girl!' said everyone, and Amanda thought she was too. And then, as she looked at the two little sixpences lying on the edge of her plate, a fine idea came to her. She could give them to

Benny for a Christmas present! He would like them very much.

So, after dinner, she took her sixpences and washed them. Then she polished them to make them bright. She went to find Benny.

'Benny,' she said, 'I didn't bring you a present because I didn't know you would be here. But now I've got one for you – my Christmas pudding sixpences! Here you are, and I wish you a happy Christmas!'

'Oh, *thank* you!' said Benny, 'but only give me one. You keep one for yourself.'

But Amanda wouldn't. She made Benny have them both, and the little boy was delighted. 'Do you know,' he said, '*no*body gave me any money this Christmas and I do like a little to spend afterwards, don't you, when our money boxes are all empty? Now I shall have Christmas money after all! It's the nicest present you could have given me!'

'I'm glad,' said Amanda, feeling very pleased. She

danced away, looking happy again. She wasn't worried any more. She had given Benny a present after all!

'I *was* lucky to get two sixpences in the Christmas pudding!' she said to herself.

And she really was, wasn't she?

First Walk in December

First Walk in December

'IT'S DECEMBER,' said Janet, looking at the calendar. 'Soon it will be Christmas!'

'Oooh – lovely!' said John, thinking of Christmas stockings, Christmas trees, and Christmas pudding.

'It's really winter now,' said Pat, looking out of the window. 'The sky is grey and heavy, the trees are bare, except for the evergreens, and the countryside looks dull and dreary. Not even Uncle Merry would find very much that is exciting.'

'We have been for two walks every month this

year,' said John. 'I've loved them. I've learnt such a lot too – things I never knew before.'

'And I've got a lot of lovely pictures stored up in my mind,' said Janet. 'Do you remember the golden buttercup fields, John? And the bees murmuring in the limes?'

'Yes – I remember,' said John. 'And I remember the blue kingfisher diving into the stream, and the lovely swallows soaring through the air.'

'And I remember old Fergus being chased by a rabbit last month,' chuckled Pat. But Janet and John flew to Fergus's defence at once.

'The rabbit was *not* chasing him. They were going round and round that oak tree, but Fergus was after the rabbit, you know he was, Pat!'

'I should just think so!' said Uncle Merry's voice, and he walked into the room with Fergus at his heels. 'Are you children ready for a walk? I've got to go away for a while before Christmas, so I may only have today to take you. Then perhaps our next walk could be on Christmas Day itself.'

'Oh, Uncle Merry, that would be lovely!' said Janet. 'Uncle Merry, Mother says will you come to Christmas dinner with us? We'd love to have you.'

'Thank you,' said Uncle Merry. 'I accept with pleasure – but is Fergus also invited?'

'Of *course*!' said John, kneeling down by the Scottie, and giving him a hug. 'As a matter of fact, Uncle Merry, we wanted *Fergus* here for Christmas, and as we couldn't get him without you, we just *had* to ask you too!' John had such a wicked twinkle in his eye as he spoke that Uncle Merry chased him all round the nursery.

'Now, now, children,' said Mother, appearing at the door. 'Really, Mr Meredith, you are as bad as the children! Have you come to take them for a walk?'

'Of course!' said Uncle Merry. 'I can't think why they are such a long time getting ready!'

Fergus scampered off to help the children to get ready. Then they all went out of the front gate and into the familiar lane. It was a cold and frosty day, and they pulled their coats and scarves warmly round them. 'Doesn't Fergus want a coat, too?' asked Janet. 'I've seen dogs wearing coats, Uncle.'

'They don't need them,' said her uncle. 'Animals grow thicker coats for the winter-time. When the spring comes I shall have to have Fergus stripped of some of his coat, or he will be too hot. Horses grow thicker coats for the winter too.'

'Animals seem to prepare well for the winter, don't they?' said John, remembering how the squirrel stored up nuts and acorns, and how the dormouse became fat and tucked himself away in a comfortable hole. 'I suppose nearly all the hibernators are asleep now, Uncle?'

'All of them,' said Uncle Merry. 'The bat hangs upside down in hollow trees or barns; the snakes are curled up together somewhere; the dormouse and the hedgehog sleep in their holes; the badger is safe in his den with his family; the frogs are in the pond and the toads under big stones. The snails are clustered together on rockeries or beneath walls, and thousands of insects are so fast asleep that you might think them dead.'

'Oh! Uncle, look – hazel catkins already!' cried John, in delight, pointing to some short green catkins growing sturdily on the hazel trees in the nearby hedge. 'Somehow they make the spring-time seem quite near!'

'Yes, it's lovely to see them in December,' said Uncle Merry. 'I always like the bareness of the trees too, much as I love the greenery of spring. You can see the beautiful shape of the trees now, and it is lovely to see even the tiniest twig clearly outlined against the sky.'

'I never thought twigs were beautiful before, but I do now,' said Janet thoughtfully, as she looked at the sharp-pointed beech twigs. 'Uncle, the beech twigs are so sharp that they really prick me when I touch the points.'

'Yes, you can always tell beech twigs by their thin, sharp buds,' said Uncle Merry. 'The horse chestnut you know because the buds are—'

'Fat and sticky!' said everyone at once.

'Yes,' said Uncle Merry, laughing; 'and see, look at the ash buds. Black as can be, bold, hard buds on the straight stem.'

'And I rather like the oak twigs too,' said Pat, looking at an oak tree that showed untidy clusters of buds here and there. 'I like the way the oak buds grow, all jumbled up – no pattern or proper arrangement. And look, Uncle – there is an oak-apple. Do you remember how I brought one to you and said it was the fruit of the oak tree as well as the acorn?'

'Yes, I remember,' said Uncle Merry. 'Well, it's a mistake shared by many other people, Pat.'

The children enjoyed trying to tell the bare trees by their twigs and trunks. The birch was easy to recognise, for it had the silvery grey bark that the children loved, and its twigs were light and graceful, waving in the wind.

'There are plenty of berries still left on the hedges for the birds,' said John. 'Look – hips and haws, Uncle, and even a few elderberries too.'

'Shall we gather some?' said Uncle Merry. 'If we are going to have a bird-table soon, we can nail twigs on to the back of it for the birds to perch on, and we could tie sprigs of berries to the twigs.'

'Oh yes,' said the children, and gathered as many berries as they could. They saw some privet berries too, on the privet hedge round the farm-garden. Uncle Merry was sure the farmer wouldn't mind them having some of those as well.

'I dried some rowan berries,' he said. 'I can put them in water to soak when we want them for our bird-table. The birds like those too.'

The rooks and jackdaws were still in the fields. Peewits stood about, and some white-winged gulls soared high in the air.

'They've come inland from the sea,' said Uncle Merry. 'Each year they seem to come farther and farther into the countryside. In London thousands come up the river Thames each year, though there was a time when not one came. Birds and animals change their customs and habits even as men do!'

'Uncle, we must take holly and mistletoe for Christmas decoration, mustn't we?' said Pat eagerly. 'There are so many holly trees round here, and they are all loaded with berries.'

'Yes, you will find plenty,' said Uncle Merry. 'Here's a beauty. Do you remember seeing the white holly flowers in the spring-time.'

The children nodded. 'Why are the leaves so very prickly?' asked John, feeling the edge of one. 'I know why they are so glossy and tough – it's to prevent the leaves from giving off too much moisture in winter-time, isn't it, Uncle?'

'Yes,' said Uncle Merry. 'Well, John, I should have thought you knew that the prickles are grown for the same reason that the hedgehog grows *his* armour – to keep away enemies that might eat him!'

'Oh yes, of course,' said John. He looked up at the top of the tree and noticed that the leaves there had few prickles, or none at all. 'I suppose the top leaves don't grow prickles because animals can't reach so high,' he thought. 'How clever trees are! They seem to think of everything!'

'Uncle, I don't expect any caterpillars feed on these tough leaves, do they?' asked Janet, picking one.

'What about the holly blue butterfly?' asked Pat, at once.

'Good boy!' said Uncle Merry, giving him a pat. 'The holly blue caterpillars *do* feed on the tough holly leaves. Good mark for *you*!'

'You won't be able to come with us and cut the holly for decoration, will you, Uncle Merry?' said Janet. 'You will be away. We'll have to come by ourselves. We'll be careful not to spoil any of the trees.'

'What about mistletoe?' asked Pat. 'Where shall we get that from, Uncle?'

'I'll show you a tree where it does not grow too high,' said Uncle Merry. 'You know that there is not a real mistletoe tree or bush, don't you? It grows on other trees, and is what we call a part-parasite, because it gets some of its food from another plant.'

Uncle Merry took them to where a clump of black poplars stood. On the poplars were many big, thick tufts of mistletoe, growing from branches. Near the poplars was an oak tree, and this too had a big tuft of mistletoe on one of its sturdy branches.

'The oak tree will be quite easy to climb,' said Uncle Merry to Pat. 'You will be able to cut a nice bunch of mistletoe from that tuft there, and take it home with you nearer Christmas-time.'

'Oh yes,' said Pat, seeing quickly how he could best climb the oak. 'Uncle Merry, how does the mistletoe grow on the oak, and on the other trees? How does it get there, to begin with?'

'The missel-thrush put it there,' said Uncle Merry, smiling to see the astonished faces of the three children. 'That's why he is called missel-thrush, because he is so fond of mistletoe berries.'

'How does he plant them?' asked John.

'Well, the mistletoe berries are very sticky,' said Uncle Merry. 'The thrush has a good feast of them, and then he wants to clean his beak. So he wipes his bill carefully on a bough, leaving behind him one or two of the sticky mistletoe seeds. These put out what are called 'sinkers' – suckers that pierce through the bark of the tree right down into the sap.'

'And then the mistletoe draws up the sap and lives on it!' said Janet. 'Very cunning!'

'Very,' said Uncle Merry. 'As soon as it has several sinkers drawing up sap, it grows a pair of sage-green leaves. The mistletoe's leaves are never the rich tender green of ordinary plants, as I expect you have already noticed. It has the dull colouring that many parasites show.'

'It gets others to do its work,' said John. 'I don't think it's a very good plant. If I were a plant, I would do my own work, and not live on others.'

'Quite right!' said Uncle Merry. 'I hope you will always feel like that.'

'Does the mistletoe have flowers?' said Janet.

'Of course,' said Uncle Merry. 'Look for them in the spring-time. Be sure to examine the pearly berries well, and see how sticky they are inside. Look for the one seed too. And don't eat either the holly or mistletoe berries, because, although the birds do so without harm, you will certainly be very sick!'

The children turned to go home after that, making a note of where the mistletoe was, so that they might come out again before Christmas and gather the decorations they needed.

'We'll get enough for Uncle Merry's house too,' said Janet to Pat, in a low tone. 'We'll decorate his study for him. He'll like that.'

The children managed to find a few flowers,

even though it was December. The usual groundsel, chickweed, and shepherd's purse were found, an unexpected red campion, and a rather small dandelion, whose golden head had no stalk at all.

'It's so afraid of the frost that it doesn't dare to grow a stalk,' said Janet. 'So I can't pick it. But there it is, Uncle, a flower in dull December!'

'We'll have to look for Christmas roses later on,' said Uncle Merry. 'We'll just have a peep at them before we go in. Do you remember finding them on our walk round the garden last January? What a long time ago that seems!'

They went in at the gate, and walked round the garden to see if there were any Christmas roses showing. There were a few stout buds uncurling their heads from the hard ground.

'They will be out by Christmas,' said Uncle Merry. 'How nice! We shall be able to give your mother a bunch of flowers from the garden.'

As they went up the garden to go indoors, the

children heard sounds of angry song, and saw two robins fighting fiercely with one another. They fell to the ground, both singing angrily, striking with their wings, and pecking hard with their sharp beaks.

'Oh! Uncle, look – why are they fighting?' asked Janet, distressed. 'I don't like it. They mustn't!'

Uncle Merry laughed. 'There won't be much harm done,' he said. 'You see, robins feed mostly on insects in the winter, besides the crumbs we give them, and there are not very many insects to be found now, as you know. So each robin likes to have his own little kingdom, his own little "beat" in which no other robin is allowed to poach.'

'How amusing!' said Janet. 'So I suppose one of those robins chose our garden for his winter kingdom, Uncle, and fought the other robin when he came poaching on it. I expect it's *your* robin that is poaching!'

One of the robins flew away, rather the worse for wear. He flew into Uncle Merry's garden, sang defiantly, and then disappeared.

'Yes, I think my garden is his kingdom,' said Uncle Merry. 'I really must apologise for his behaviour. Fergus, I sincerely trust that *you* will never behave like that!'

Fergus panted and wagged his tail. 'He says, "How *could* you think such a thing!"' said Janet, with a laugh. 'Goodbye, Uncle Merry. See you at Christmas-time. You *will* come back for Christmas, won't you?'

'Of course,' said Uncle Merry, jumping over his garden wall and landing safely in his garden. 'And remember – don't wait for *me* to take you for walks. Go for some by yourselves, and when I come back, tell me all you've seen.'

'We will,' promised the children, and indoors they ran, glad to see the big playroom fire gleaming and dancing in welcome.

The Christmas-Tree Fairy

The Christmas-Tree Fairy

ONCE UPON a time old Dame Trit-trot went to market and bought a big spray of holly berries to make her house pretty. And when she got home, what did she find fast asleep in the middle of the prickly spray, but a small fairy, wrapped in a cobweb blanket!

Now Dame Trit-trot did not believe in fairies at all, so, of course, she did not think this was a fairy.

'It's a doll!' she said. 'How strange! Well, I never saw such a dainty little doll before! It will do for my granddaughter Jane.'

So she wrapped the fairy in white tissue-paper and put her in a cardboard box. She took it to Jane the next day, and Jane opened the box and unwrapped the tissue-paper.

Jane's mother peeped into the box and saw the sleeping fairy there. 'Oh!' she cried, 'what a beautiful little doll! It has wings like a fairy.'

'It *is* a fairy,' said Jane, who believed in fairies, and knew one when she saw one.

'Don't be silly, darling,' said her mother. 'There are no such things as fairies!'

'But, Mother, this is a real live one!' cried Jane. 'It is, it is! Look at her wings! Look at her tiny little nails!'

'What funny things children say!' said Granny Trit-trot. So Jane said no more. But she knew quite well that the doll was a real live fairy, fast asleep.

She carried the box away to her nursery and took out the sleeping fairy very carefully. She put her into her doll's bed and covered her up well. How lovely the fairy looked, lying in the tiny bed, her golden hair fluffed out on the little pillow, and one of her small hands outside the sheet. Jane was so happy and excited. When would the fairy wake up?

'Jane, Jane! Here's John come to see you!' Mother called up the stairs – and Jane heard John running up. She ran to meet him, her face red with excitement.

'John! Come here! I've got a real live fairy asleep in my doll's bed! Look!'

She took John to the bed and he looked down at the sleeping fairy. Then he laughed. 'That's only a doll!' he said. 'I don't believe in fairies, Jane. That's a doll – you can't make me believe it's a fairy!'

'But look at her silvery wings peeping out of the bedclothes!' said Jane. 'Look at her beautiful hair! Besides, she is alive. Don't you see her pink cheeks?'

'It's just a Christmas-tree fairy doll,' said John. 'I tell you, I don't believe in fairies!'

Jane said no more. She knew that Angela, her friend, believed in fairies, so that afternoon she made

Angela come in from her walk and see the doll.

'Jane! It's a real live fairy!' said Angela, in delight. 'Oh, Jane, how lucky you are! How lucky!'

'Isn't it funny, Angela, people who don't believe in fairies think she's just a doll,' said Jane. 'So they only see a doll lying there – but you and I, who do believe in fairies, can see quite well that she is really a sleeping fairy! Oh, I do wonder when she will wake up!'

Every day Jane went to the doll's bed to see if the fairy had awakened – but not until the day of the Christmas party came did the little fairy open her eyes! She had had such a long sleep! How surprised she was to find herself tucked up cosily on a soft little bed!

'Oh!' cried Jane, when she saw the fairy sit up and rub her eyes. 'I knew you were a fairy, and not a doll!'

The two talked together, and Jane told the fairy that her mother had said it would be nice to put the fairy at the top of the Christmas-tree that evening. 'You see, Mother thinks you are only a fairy doll,' said

Jane. 'She doesn't believe in fairies. Will you mind standing at the top of the tree, fairy?'

'Not a bit,' said the fairy. 'And I'll give each child who believes in me a wish to wish – one that will come true! So you must tell all those who don't believe in fairies to go out of the room, Jane – and I will fly down and hear every child's wish. And then, dear Jane, I must fly away. This is a dear soft little bed, but I have my own home, you know. I will often come and see you again.'

'Ssh!' said Jane. 'Here comes Mother.'

Jane's mother carried the fairy doll to the Christmas-tree and put her at the top. How pretty she looked there!

'It's the loveliest fairy doll I've ever seen!' said Mother.

In the middle of the party, when the Christmas-tree was shining with candles, Jane clapped her hands and made everyone quiet.

'Please, will you do something for me?' she said.

'Will everyone who doesn't believe in fairies go out of the room – and all those who *do* believe in them stay here with me? I have a secret to show to them!'

All the grown-ups except Aunt Susan went out. Two little girls and three boys went out, too. Alan, Mollie, Angela, Trixie, Jack, and Jane were left.

'I know your secret!' cried Jack. 'It's the doll up there! She's a Christmas-tree fairy – a real live one! I saw her smiling at us just now!'

'Yes – that's my secret,' said Jane. 'She is going to fly down to each of you and give you a wish. Keep still and think hard what you would like most!'

Each child stood still – and the little fairy flew down on her silvery wings. She listened to every child's wish and nodded her golden head. 'It will come true!' she said.

And then she flew out of the window and disappeared into the dark night. 'She has gone back to her home,' said Jane.

When the other children and grown-ups came back,

they were surprised to see no doll at the top of the Christmas-tree! 'Where is she?' they cried.

'She has flown out of the window!' said Jane.

But, you know, they didn't believe her. Do tell me – would you have been *out*side the door – or *in*side – if you had been at Jane's Christmas party?

A Christmas Legend

A Christmas Legend

ONCE UPON a time, in the ivied tower of a little church there were three wonderful bells. They rang only on Christmas Eve when the people brought their gifts to church, to be given to the poor in remembrance of the Christ Child. Nobody knew who rang them. Some said it was the wind, some said it was the angels, and some that they rang at God's own bidding. Be that as it may, every year the bells pealed forth their welcome to all who loved the Christ Child.

But there came a year when the Christmas bells were silent. The people waited and waited for the familiar peal, but not a sound broke the stillness. The next year it was the same, and so it was for many years.

'What has happened to our bells, our wonderful Christmas bells?' the sorrowing people asked. 'Shall we never hear their music again?'

At last the Father of the Church asked all to bring their choicest gifts. 'For,' he said, 'perhaps our gifts have not been worthy of the Christ Child, and that is why the bells do not ring.'

So, on Christmas Eve, when a myriad of stars shone down upon the snowy earth, the people made their way to church, bearing their most precious gifts. Among them were two ragged little boys whose present was a silver ten-pence piece. They had struggled for a whole year to save this, and how proud they were of it now, and how glad to give it to the Christ Child! They smiled as they trudged along in the snow, saying little, but each thinking his own happy thoughts.

Suddenly they were stopped in their way by an old, old man, far poorer than they. In a voice that trembled from weariness and hunger, he asked, 'Little brothers, can you spare a penny for a poor old man who has nothing?'

The boys looked at the old man and their hearts were filled with pity. But how could they help him? They had no penny but only their silver piece, and if they gave him this, what of their gift for the Christ Child?

The problem puzzled them. But when they looked again at the poor man, shivering in his rags, they were so moved with pity for him that they gave him all their money.

The old man was overcome with joy at the magnificence of their gift. 'May God bless you for this, little brothers,' he said. And with a last, long look of gratitude he bade them farewell and shuffled away in the snow.

The boys went on, and although now they had no gift for the Christ Child they knew in their hearts that God would understand, for wasn't the poor old man also His child?

They reached the church at last, and as they stepped into its welcoming light they heard the Father inviting all to bring their presents and lay them before the altar. 'And God grant,' he added, 'that we may hear once more the music of our Christmas bells.'

The people brought their gifts and laid them before the altar. Princes gave their jewelled crowns, and ladies gave their rings; the rich gave ornaments of priceless worth, and merchants gave their gold. But still the bells were silent.

Last of all came the two little ragged boys who, in loving kindness, had given away all they had. They knelt down side by side before the altar and held out their empty hands. Immediately the Christmas bells began to ring, louder and sweeter than ever before.

'Thine is the gift divine – thine is the gift divine,' they seemed to sing, and sing again.

Those who had given of their plenty knelt down in all humility, and with tears of joy in their eyes gave thanks to God for the music of the Christmas Bells.

Ring-a-ding-ding,
Ring-a-ding-ding,
Can you hear the bells –
The merry Christmas bells?
'Peace on earth,' they ring,
'Goodwill to men,' they sing;
'Peace on earth, goodwill to men,'
They ring and sing again –
The merry Christmas bells,
The merry Christmas bells.

The Christmas Bicycle

The Christmas Bicycle

TESSIE HAD a bicycle for Christmas, and all the other boys and girls thought she was very lucky, because it really was a nice one.

At first she lent it to anyone who wanted to try and ride it, but when Harry had dented the mudguard, and Jane had broken a pedal, Tessie's mother said she was not to lend it to any child except in her own garden.

Susan was cross when she heard this. 'Oh, how mean of your mother!' she said. 'She might let you lend it in the road, Tessie!'

'Mother isn't mean,' said Tessie, who would never let anyone say a word against her mother. 'It's just that she paid a lot of money for my bike, and she doesn't want it spoilt. She's not mean.'

'Well, you ask me to tea and then I can ride your bike in the garden,' said Susan. So Tessie told her mother that Susan wanted to come to tea so that she could ride the bicycle.

'Susan always wants to push in and get her own way,' said Tessie's mother. 'No, I can't have her to tea just yet, Tessie. You are having your cousin for the day this week, and Harry is coming to tea on Tuesday. You can't have Susan.'

Susan was cross. 'Well, I said it before and I say it again – your mother is mean!' she said to Tessie.

Tessie walked off without a word. She was not going to quarrel with Susan, but she wasn't going to stay with her if she said things like that.

Susan soon tried to make Tessie friends with her again, because she so badly wanted to ride Tessie's bicycle. So she gave her a sweet, and told her that she was the nicest girl in the class. When Tessie was sucking the sweet and was nice and friendly once more, Susan asked for a ride.

'Let me have a little ride, just a tiny little ride on your bike,' she said. 'We'll wait till all the other boys and girls have gone, Tessie, then no one will see. I'll ride it down the lane, that's all. Please do let me.'

'Mother said I wasn't to,' said Tessie.

'Well,' said Susan, thinking of another idea, 'well, Tessie, you just turn your back for a minute – and I'll hop on the bike and ride off without you seeing. Then it won't matter, because, you see, you won't have *lent* me the bike; I shall have taken it. Please, please, do let me have a ride, Tessie. You're so lucky to have a bike.'

'Well,' said Tessie, hardly liking to say no, because she saw how much Susan wanted a ride, 'well – just this once, then.'

She turned her back. Susan jumped on to the bike and rode away down the lane. How fast she rode! How grand she felt!

Just as she passed a field-gate a cow came out,

the first of a herd driven out by the farmer. Susan got a fright, wobbled, and fell off. Crash! She fell on her side and grazed her arm badly, and tore her frock.

Tessie heard the crash and turned. She ran to Susan and helped her up. 'Oh, I knew I shouldn't have let you ride my bike,' she said. 'I knew I shouldn't! Look at your poor arm – and what will your mother say to your torn frock?'

The bicycle was not hurt, which was lucky. Susan picked it up, brushed her frock down, and looked at her bleeding arm. 'Bother!' she said. 'That tiresome cow! It made me fall off.'

'Well, you shouldn't have been on the bike, should you, really?' said Tessie, taking it. 'You shouldn't have told me to turn my head away so that you could take it without my seeing you. It's a good thing the bike isn't damaged. Mother *would* have been cross with you – and with me, too, for disobeying her.'

Susan went home, trying to hide her torn frock and grazed arm. But her mother saw them both at once.

'Susan! What have you done to your arm? Did you fall down? And how did you tear your frock?'

'I was riding Tessie's bike,' said Susan, not liking to tell her mother a story. 'A cow came out of a gate and scared me, and I fell off.'

'Susan, you are *not* to ride other people's bicycles,' said her mother at once; 'for two reasons – one is that you may damage someone else's bike, and the other is that you haven't had enough practice in riding, and until you have you are not to ride in the road. You might have a bad accident.'

'I shouldn't,' said Susan, looking sulky.

'Now, do you understand, Susan?' said her mother. 'I mean it. You are *not* to ride Tessie's bicycle, or anyone else's. One day you shall have one of your own, and then you can practise riding it round and round your own garden till you can ride well enough to go out into the road. Be patient and wait till then.'

Susan didn't feel at all patient. How could she wait, perhaps for years, for a bicycle? She knew that a bicycle was expensive, and she knew that her mother hadn't a lot of money to spare. She might have to wait till she was twelve before she had a bicycle – and she wasn't even nine till next week! How she wished she could have a bicycle for her ninth birthday! That would be grand.

Her arm soon healed. Her dress was mended. Once or twice her mother warned her to remember what she had said about Tessie's bicycle.

'You will remember that I don't want you to ride Tessie's bicycle again, won't you?' she said. 'And I hear that Tessie's mother has asked her not to lend it to anyone, too – so on no account must you borrow it, Susan.'

Susan didn't say anything. She meant to have another ride whenever she could! Her mother noticed that she said noting and spoke sharply.

'Susan! Will you promise me not to ride on Tessie's bicycle?' she said.

'All right,' said Susan, sulkily. How tiresome to

have to promise! 'I wish I could have a bike for my birthday next week, Mother. Tessie was only nine when she had hers.'

'Bicycles are so expensive,' said Susan's mother; 'and you are not very old yet. There is plenty of time for you to have a bicycle, Susan!'

Susan didn't ask Tessie for a ride any more that week. She watched her riding to and from school very enviously, but she didn't beg for a turn too. She didn't want to upset Tessie, or to break her own promise.

The next week came. The day before her birthday came. Susan told everyone it was her birthday the next day, and she felt excited because she knew Mother was making her a cake with nine candles on it, and she thought she was having a workbasket and a new book, too. Now, as Susan went home from school that afternoon, she suddenly saw Tessie's bicycle leaning against the wall that ran round Harry's garden in the main road! Yes, there it was, bright and shining. Tessie must have gone in to see Harry's white mice.

'The road's empty. I'll just jump on Tessie's bike and have a little ride!' thought Susan. 'No one will know. I'll go round the corner and back.'

Quite forgetting her promise, Susan jumped on the bicycle and rode down the road. She went fast, pedalling up and down strongly. She rang her bell at the corner. *Ting-a-ling-a-ling!* It sounded fine. Then she put the brakes on to see if they worked. But they didn't work very well. Tessie had been told that she must take her bicycle to the shop to have the brakes put right, or else she might have an accident.

'Now I'd better go back,' thought Susan to herself, and turned to go back. She had pedalled up the hill, and now it would be fun to go down it without pedalling at all!

She simply *flew* down! It was quite a steep hill. Suddenly, round the corner, came the big old cart-horse belonging to the farmer, dragging a heavy cart behind him.

Susan wobbled. She rang her bell, but the horse

took no notice. She put on the brakes to slow the bicycle down – but they didn't work! The bicycle flew on and on, and it seemed as if the big horse and cart blocked up the whole of the road. Just as she reached the horse, Susan tried to jump off the bike. But it was going too fast for her to jump properly. She slipped, the bicycle flew straight into the alarmed horse, and Susan herself rolled over and over and over towards the side of the road. She sat up, gasping, looking at herself to see if she was hurt. But she wasn't! There didn't seem even to be a bruise or a scratch.

Then she looked round for the bicycle. But, oh, what a pity; it was completely spoilt! The frightened horse had reared up when Susan had run into it, and brought its heavy, enormous hoofs down on to the bicycle. The wheels were buckled and broken. The handle was twisted. The right pedal was off and the left one was broken.

'Oh! Look at Tessie's bike!' said Susan, with tears in her eyes. The farmer was trying to pull it from his horse's feet. He thought the bicycle was Susan's.

'I'm afraid your bike's done for, missy,' he said. 'Why did you ride so fast down the hill? That was silly of you. You frightened my horse terribly. He might have run away.'

Susan didn't know what to do. Crying bitterly, she dragged the poor, broken bike home at last, and her mother came running out to see whatever was the matter.

'Oh, Mother – oh, Mother – look at Tessie's bike!' wept Susan. 'I broke my promise. I took it when Tessie was at Harry's – and I ran into a horse, and the horse stamped on the bike. Oh, Mother, what shall I do?'

Mother looked in horror at the bicycle. 'Are you hurt?' she said to Susan. Susan shook her head. 'Well, you might easily have been killed, Susan. And *look* at Tessie's bike! Whatever will her father and mother say?'

'I don't know, I don't know!' wailed Susan.

'Oh, why did I disobey you and break my promise, Mother?'

Susan's mother looked very grave. She set the broken bicycle by the fence, and took Susan's arm. 'Come with me,' she said. 'I will show you what you must do.'

She took Susan to a shed, which was locked. She unlocked it. Inside was a brand-new, very beautiful shining new bicycle! Susan gave a gasp when she saw it.

'Look,' said Mother. 'Daddy and I bought this for your birthday tomorrow, for a big surprise. Now, Susan, I am afraid you must take it to Tessie instead, because you have completely spoilt *her* bicycle. Maybe we can get Tessie's mended up for you – I don't know – but you will certainly have to give up your new bicycle to Tessie.'

Oh, what a pity! Oh, what a terrible pity to have to give up such a beautiful bicycle to somebody else, all because of a moment's disobedience and a broken promise! How Susan cried! How she wept and wailed! But she knew Mother was right. It was the only thing to do.

So now Tessie has Susan's beautiful bicycle, and Susan is waiting to hear if Tessie's old one can be mended at all. Poor Susan – it was very hard for her, wasn't it? But, as Mother said, you never know *what* may happen if you are disobedient or break a solemn promise!

A Grand Visitor

A Grand Visitor

NOW ONCE there was great excitement in Toyland because a grand visitor was expected. He was to stay at the toy castle up on the hill.

'He comes once a year,' said Bruiny to Tiptoe. 'Guess who it is!'

But Tiptoe couldn't. 'Well, I'll tell you,' said Bruiny, feeling most important because he knew something that Tiptoe and Jolly didn't know. 'It's Father Christmas!'

'*Really*!' cried Tiptoe, surprised. 'What does he come here for?'

'Can't you guess, silly?' cried Bruiny. 'He comes to

get toys from Toyland to put into his sack, to take to children.'

Tiptoe and Jolly looked rather frightened. They had once belonged to children. They had been in a nursery where the other toys had been unkind to them, so they had run away together to Toyland. Now the very idea of going back to a nursery filled them with alarm. What – leave dear little Jolly Cottage and go right away? And suppose Tiptoe was taken to one house and Jolly to another? Suppose they never saw one another again?

But all the other toys thought it was a great adventure to go into Father Christmas's sack and be taken to the world of children. They talked about nothing else all day long. How they hoped they would be chosen!

Toy Town itself began to be very crowded and busy as the day drew near for Father Christmas to come. All the balls from Roll-About Town came along, rolling and bouncing in glee, wondering if they would be put into somebody's stocking.

The big rocking horses came too, rocking themselves down the streets. Nobody liked them very much, because they were so big and didn't always look where they were going.

The humming tops came with their beautiful hums. They spun down the streets and looked out for Father Christmas. Toy motor cars whizzed along; toy rabbits, cats and dogs ran about with new ribbons round their necks. It really was most exciting.

Everyone was happy and excited except poor Jolly and Tiptoe. They simply couldn't bear to think that they might be taken away from dear old Toyland and all their friends. They shut themselves up in their cottage and wondered if they dared to stay there all the time that Father Christmas was visiting Toyland.

'If we stay in our cottage he won't see us and then he can't choose us to go into his sack,' said Jolly.

So they stayed inside Jolly Cottage and didn't go out at all, except when they had to fetch food from the market. And one morning, as they were buying carrots and onions, there was a great commotion.

'Father Christmas is coming! He's coming!' shouted Mr To-and-Fro, wobbling so much that he almost knocked Tiptoe over. 'Hark! Can you hear his sleigh-bells?'

Tiptoe and Jolly couldn't get out of the crowd. They stood trembling there, hoping that Father Christmas wouldn't see them. Then along came a fine sleigh drawn by four reindeer, tossing their fine antlers in the air. And there was jolly old Father Christmas sitting in the sleigh, holding the reins in one hand and waving to everyone with the other. At his side was an enormous sack, quite empty.

'See his sack? That will be full of toys when he leaves tonight!' whispered Mr To-and-Fro. 'I wonder if you or Jolly will be in it, Tiptoe.'

Tiptoe turned pale. 'Please let's go home, Jolly,' she said.

Father Christmas went by. He caught sight of

the sailor doll and the little fairy doll, and waved to them. Jolly waved back, but Tiptoe didn't. She really felt quite ill.

As soon as Jolly could get out of the crowd, he took Tiptoe's arm and hurried her away. They went up the hill and into their little cottage. Jolly shut the door and locked it. He shut the windows, too.

'I like Father Christmas very much,' he said to Tiptoe. 'But I couldn't just bear him to take either of us away, Tiptoe. Now, don't cry. We are safe here.'

The two dolls stayed at home all day. They did not know what was going on at all. They heard shouts and cheers, but they did not even go to the window to look down the hill.

Father Christmas was giving a grand party. Everyone was there, down to the smallest ball. Josie, Click and Bun were there, and they looked about for Tiptoe and Jolly, and wondered where they could be.

At the end of the party came the grand Choosing Time. Every toy had to march past Father Christmas and he said whether or not he would have them for his sack.

Only balls that bounced well, only tops that hummed properly, toy animals that were quite perfect, and dolls that looked happy and smiley were chosen.

Father Christmas was up in the big toy castle, sitting on his throne, his red cloak flowing out round him. He sat there, big and jolly, making jokes as the toys marched by.

'You, little red ball, come along into my sack! You'll go into the foot of a stocking very nicely!'

And the little red ball, with a bounce of excitement, rolled into the enormous sack that Father Christmas was holding open.

'And you, baby doll, come along in!' cried Father Christmas. 'I know a little girl called Ann who will love to have you. And you, humming top, spin into my sack! I've a boy on my list called Michael, he'll love to spin you and hear you hum! And you, blue cat, come into my sack. I'll take you to a small girl called Shirley.'

So the toys marched or rolled or spun into the big sack. And when all of them had passed by, Father Christmas looked a bit puzzled.

'That's strange,' he said. 'I thought I saw a pretty fairy doll and a jolly sailor doll this morning. I would have liked to take them with me. Are they here?'

'No, they're not,' said Mr To-and-Fro, looking all round. 'But I know where they live. I will get them.' So he wobbled off as fast as he could and was soon knocking on the door of Jolly Cottage. When he told the two dolls what he had come for, they looked very frightened and miserable.

But they had to go with Mr To-and-Fro. Soon they were standing in front of Father Christmas, and he smiled at them.

'Cheer up, dolls! I've some good news for you! I'm going to take you with me! March into my sack – and then I must go!'

So poor Tiptoe and Jolly had to march into the big open sack, which was now almost full to the top with toys of all kinds. Father Christmas closed the neck of the sack and swung it over his shoulder.

'Goodbye, Toys!' he said cheerfully. 'See you again next year. Happy Christmas!'

And off he went to his reindeer sleigh, his sack over his shoulder. He got in, took the reins and clicked to his reindeer. 'Jingle-jingle,' the bells rang as the reindeer set out for the gates of Toyland.

'We're leaving dear Toyland behind,' whispered Jolly, his eyes full of tears.

'We shan't see our dear little cottage any more,' wept Tiptoe.

'We didn't say goodbye to Bruiny or the clockwork clown,' sobbed Jolly. 'Oh, I'm so unhappy. I know you will go to one home and I shall go to another. We shall never, never see one another again. Oh, Tiptoe, I'm so miserable!'

Now the two toys were near the top of the sack,

which was still over Father Christmas's shoulder. Their tears trickled out and fell down his neck. He felt them, wet and warm, and was most astonished.

'Where's this water coming from? he wondered. 'It's not raining!' He stopped his reindeer and opened the sack. Out fell Tiptoe and Jolly, still weeping bitterly. Father Christmas stared in surprise.

'What's the matter?' he asked at last. 'Aren't you pleased to be going with me?'

'Oh, Father Christmas, we've both been in a nursery before,' said Jolly, wiping his eyes and trying to be brave, in case Father Christmas was cross with him. 'And we weren't happy, so we ran away to Toyland, and we've got such a dear little cottage and we were so happy.'

'And now we have got to say goodbye to one another, and we just can't bear it!' sobbed poor Tiptoe.

'Dear me! Why didn't you tell me you had been out in the big world before and had lived in a nursery?' asked Father Christmas. 'Don't you know that toys are only allowed to go out into the world once? There aren't enough adventures to go round more than once, you know. You are taking somebody else's turn!'

'Oh, we didn't know, we didn't know!' cried Jolly. 'May we go home again then? Oh, may we?'

'You'll have to,' said Father Christmas, smiling kindly at them. 'Off you go. We're at the gates of Toyland, so you'll have to walk a good way home. But I don't expect you'll mind that!'

'Goodbye!' said Jolly and Tiptoe, scrambling out of the big sleigh. 'Goodbye – and thank you very much!'

'Jingle-jingle' – the reindeer sped out of the gates of Toyland, and left Jolly and Tiptoe standing there by themselves. They flung their arms round one another in joy. 'We're still together after all!' said Jolly, wiping away Tiptoe's tears. 'Cheer up. We'll soon be back at Jolly Cottage. And won't everyone be glad to see us!'

So back they went – and oh, how sweet their little

house looked, as they came up the hill! How glad everyone was to see them back!

'It's lovely to be home again,' said Jolly, as he unlocked the door. 'Now, Tiptoe, we'll live happily here for ever after. You just see if we don't!'

And I expect they will, don't you?

The Little Carol-Singer

The Little Carol-Singer

'WHAT'S THE matter with John?' said Grandfather in surprise. 'He does look miserable!'

'Well, he's got a cold, and so he can't go out carol-singing with the school choir,' said John's mother. 'He's upset because he does so love carols – and he's got a lovely voice, you know.'

'Yes, I know,' said Grandfather. 'So had I when I was a boy like John. Tell John to come along to me. I've got something to tell him.'

John came, and went over to his grandfather. The old man put his arm round him and smiled. 'So you are disappointed because you can't go carol-singing.

What carols were you going to sing?'

'Oh – lovely ones: "Good King Wenceslas", and "Nowell, Nowell", and "The Holy Babe" – and "Here We Come A-wassailing". I love that one,' said John. 'I don't know what "wassailing" means, though.'

'It means a merry party, where wassail was drunk,' said his grandfather. 'It's a very old carol, you know. I used to sing it as a boy too. I remember one time very well indeed.'

'Tell me about it, Grandfather,' said John. He liked to hear the old man's stories of his long-ago boyhood.

'Well,' said Grandfather, 'I was about six years old, I suppose, and it was wintertime, very cold and frosty. There were my mother and I and my little sister Hannah, all living in a tiny cottage together.'

'Where was your father?' asked John.

'He was dead,' said Grandfather. 'He left my mother a little money but it soon went – and that winter, when Christmas was near, my poor mother couldn't even pay the rent of the little cottage.'

'What happened?' asked John. 'Was she turned out?'

'The landlord was a hard man,' said his grandfather. 'He said that unless she could find some money to give him, she must be turned out of her cottage with my little sister and I. We had nowhere to go, and it was bitter weather. I remember my mother crying.'

'What did you do?' asked John.

'Well, I made up my mind that *I* must get some money somehow,' said Grandfather. 'So I put on my cap and coat and out I went into the snow. But nobody wanted a little boy's work! Nobody wanted snow swept away, or errands run. I didn't get a single penny.'

'Poor Grandfather,' said John. 'I would have given you everything in my moneybox. Yes, even my bright new pound coin!'

'I began to trudge home in the snow, cold and hungry,' went on the old man. 'I even remember how numb my hands were and how I put them under my armpits to try and warm them. And then, as it grew dark, I heard the sound of singing.'

'What was it? Carol-singers?' asked John.

'Yes. It was a party of villagers, going from house to house, singing all kinds of carols,' said Grandfather. 'In those days the big houses threw open their doors to the singers, and welcomed them in, and gave them mulled wine and spiced apples, and little cakes.'

'That sounds nice,' said John. 'I should like a spiced apple. What did you do next, Grandfather? Please tell me.'

'I thought of the spiced apples and little cakes,' said Grandfather. 'And I was so hungry that I felt I really must have something to eat. So I joined the party of carol-singers, without being seen, and went with them up the long drive to the Squire's house.'

'Were you found out?' asked John.

'I sang with them,' said Grandfather, remembering that long ago evening clearly. 'We sang "The Holy Babe". I remember then the door opened, and the

Squire himself welcomed us in. I went in too, scared but so cold and hungry that I longed to see a fire, and have something to eat.'

'Was there a nice fire?' said John.

'An enormous one,' went on Grandfather. 'It was blazing up in the big hall. The Squire's lady was there, pretty and kind and smiling – and on a big table there were jugs of warm drinks, and dishes of spiced apples and plates of little cakes. I could hardly take my eyes off them. But before we could eat and drink, we had to sing again.'

'What did you sing?' asked John.

'The carol you said you liked,' said his grandfather. '"Here We Come A-wassailing". I sang too, because I knew the words and the tune. And I remember the villagers turning to stare at me and wondering how I came to be with them. I remember the Squire's lady looking at me, and listening to my voice. And at the end she said, "Little boy, you have a very sweet voice. I would like to hear you sing by yourself."'

'Oh Grandfather – what happened then?' asked John.

'I sang the chorus of "Here We Come A-wassailing," said Grandfather, 'and everyone listened, because in those days I had a lovely voice. And then the Squire's lady gave me something hot to drink, and a spiced apple and two little cakes. I drank my drink and ate the spiced apple – but I put the cakes into my pocket.'

'Why? To take home?' asked John.

'Yes. For my mother and sister,' said Grandfather. 'But one of the villagers saw me stuffing the cakes into my pocket and he was angry. I think he thought I had taken them from the table when nobody was looking. He began to scold me – and what with the hot drink, and the blazing fire, and the thought of going home to my mother without anything at all to give her, I suddenly found tears pouring down my cheeks. I was so ashamed. I tried to stumble to the door and go.'

'Did they let you?' asked John. 'Poor Grandfather! What a horrid ending to your evening!'

'Oh, that wasn't the end,' said Grandfather. 'The Squire's lady jumped up, put her arms round me and led me to a seat by the fire. "Now you tell me why you are sad," she said. "A boy with a voice like yours shouldn't be sad! He should be glad!"'

'She was nice,' said John.

'So I told her everything,' said Grandfather. 'About my mother and sister, and how we had no money and how the next day we were all to be turned out in the snow. I told her I had no right to be with the carol-singers, or to eat her apples and cakes. But by that time the others had gone on their way and I was left with the Squire and his lady.'

'Go on, Grandfather,' begged John. 'This is a much nicer ending! It is all true, isn't it?'

'Oh yes!' said Grandfather. 'Quite true. The Squire took me home to my mother, and told her that he had a fine little cottage she could go to the next day, and pay no rent for – but he wanted one thing in return.'

'What was it?' asked John.

'He wanted my mother to let me learn singing and music, and to have my voice trained – and he said that when I grew up and earned money by my voice and music, then I could pay him back,' said Grandfather. 'My mother could hardly believe her ears!'

'Oh, Grandfather – and that was how you became such a famous singer and musician!' cried John. 'All because you went carolling one night, hungry and cold!'

'Yes. So now you know why, like you, I love the old carol, "Here We Come A-wassailing",' said Grandfather. 'Let's call Mother and go to the piano and sing it together, shall we? And I shall remember again the time when I too went "wassailing" years and years ago!'

The Man
Who Wasn't
Father Christmas

The Man Who Wasn't Father Christmas

THERE WAS once an old man with a long white beard who loved children. He was very poor, so he couldn't give the children anything, and you can guess that he always wished at Christmas-time that he was Father Christmas.

'Goodness! What fun I'd have if I were Father Christmas!' he thought. 'Think of having a sack that was always full of toys that couldn't be emptied, because it was magic. How happy I should be!'

Now one Christmas-time the old man saw a little notice in the window of a big shop. This is what it said:

'WANTED. A man with a white beard to be Father Christmas, and give out paper leaflets in the street.'

Well, the old man stared at this notice, and wondered if he could get the job. How lovely to dress up as Father Christmas, and go up and down the streets with all the children staring at him! He would be so happy.

So he marched into the shop and asked if he could have the job.

'The work is not hard,' said the shopman. 'All you have to do is to dress up in a red cloak and trousers and big boots, and take a sack with you.'

'Will it be full of toys?' asked the old man, his eyes shining at the thought.

'Of course not!' said the shopman. 'It will be full of leaflets for you to give to the passers-by. I have had these leaflets printed to tell everyone to come to our shop this Christmas and buy their presents here. I thought it would be a good idea to dress somebody up as Father Christmas, and let him give out the leaflets.'

'I see,' said the old man. 'I rather thought it would be nice to give the children something.'

'Well, what an idea!' said the shop-man. 'Now, see if this red Father Christmas costume fits you.'

It fitted the old man well. He got into it and looked at himself in the glass. He really looked exactly like old Father Christmas. His long white beard flowed down over his chest and his bright blue eyes twinkled brightly.

He took his sack of leaflets and went out. It was the day before Christmas and everyone was busy shopping. How the children stared when they saw the old man walking along in the road!

'It's Father Christmas!' they shouted. 'It's Father Christmas! Come and see him!'

Soon the children were crowding round the old man, asking if they could peep into his sack. But alas, there were no toys there, and all he had to give the children were the leaflets. The children were disappointed.

'Fancy Father Christmas only giving us leaflets about Mr White's shop,' they said. 'We thought he was a kind old man – but he isn't. He didn't even give us a sweet.'

The old man heard the children saying these things and he was sad. 'I made a mistake in taking this job,' he said to himself. 'It is horrid to pretend to be somebody kind and not be able to give the boys and girls even a penny! I feel dreadful!'

It began to snow. The old man plodded along the streets, giving out his leaflets. And suddenly he heard a curious sound. It was the sound of bells!

'Where are those bells, I wonder?' thought the old man, looking all round. 'It sounds like horse-bells. But everyone has cars nowadays. There are no horses in this town.'

It wasn't horse-bells he heard. It was reindeer-bells! To the great surprise of the old man, a large sleigh drove down the road, drawn by reindeer. And in it was – well, you can guess without being told – the *real* Father Christmas!

The sleigh drew up, and Father Christmas leaned out. 'Am I anywhere near the town of Up-and-Down?' he called. Then he stared hard at the old man – and he frowned.

'You look like *me!*' he said. 'Why are you dressed like that?'

'Well, just to get a job of work,' said the old man. 'But really because I love children, and I thought if I dressed up like you, they would think I *was* you, and would come round me and be happy. But all I have in my sack is stupid leaflets about somebody's shop – I haven't any toys to give away, as you have. So instead of making the children happy I have disappointed them. I am sorry now I ever took this job.'

'Well, well, you did it for the best,' said Father Christmas, smiling suddenly. 'I like people who love children. They are always the nicest people, you know. Look here – would you like to do me a good turn?'

'I'd love to,' said the old man.

'Well,' said Father Christmas, 'I haven't had any tea, and I feel so hungry and thirsty. Would you mind taking care of my reindeer for me whilst I'm in a tea-shop? They don't like standing still, so you'll have to drive them round and round the town. And if you meet any children, you must do exactly as I always do.'

'What's that?' asked the old man, his eyes shining.

'You must stop, and say to them, "A happy Christmas to you! What would you like out of my sack?" And you must let the child dip its hand into my sack and take out what it wants. You won't mind doing that, will you? I always do that as I drive along.'

'*Mind* doing that! It would be the thing I would like best in the world,' said the old man, hardly believing his ears. 'It's – it's – it's – well, I just can't tell you how happy it will make me. I can't believe it's true!'

Father Christmas smiled his wide smile. He jumped down from the sleigh and threw the reins to the old man.

'Come back in an hour,' he said. 'I'll have finished my tea by then.'

He went into a tea-shop. The old man climbed into the driving-seat. He was trembling with joy. He looked at the enormous sack beside him on the seat. It was simply bursting with toys! He cracked the whip and the reindeer set off with a jingling of bells.

Soon they met three children. How those children stared! Then they went quite mad with delight and yelled to the old man: 'Father Christmas! Father Christmas! Stop a minute, do!'

The old man stopped the reindeer. He beamed at the children. 'A happy Christmas to you!' he said. 'What would you like out of my sack?'

'An engine, please,' said the boy.

'A doll, please,' said one of the girls.

'A book, please,' said another girl.

'Dip into my sack and find what you want,' said the old man. And with shining faces the three children dipped in their hands – and each of them pulled out exactly what he wanted! They rushed home with shouts of joy.

Well, the old man stopped at every child he met, wished them a happy Christmas, and asked them what they wanted. And dozens of happy children dipped into the enormous sack and pulled out just what they longed for.

At the end of an hour the old man drove the reindeer back to the tea-shop. Father Christmas was waiting, putting on his big fur gloves. He smiled when he saw the bright face of the old man.

'You've had a good time, I can see,' he said. 'Thanks so much. I don't give presents to grown-ups usually – but you might hang up your stocking just for fun tonight. Goodbye!'

He drove off with a ringing of sleigh-bells. The old man went back to the shop in a happy dream, took off his red clothes and went home.

'I've never been so happy before,' he said as he got into bed. 'Never! If only people knew how wonderful it is to give happiness to others! How lucky Father Christmas is to go about the world giving presents to all the boys and girls!'

The old man hung up his stocking, though he felt rather ashamed of it. And when he woke up in the morning, what do you think was in it?

A magic purse was in it – a purse that was always full of pennies! No matter how many were taken out, there were always some left.

'A penny-purse – a magic penny-purse!' cried the old man joyfully. 'My word – what fun I'll have with the children now!'

He does – for he always has a penny to give each one. I wonder if you've ever seen the little penny-purse. It is black and has two letters in silver on the front. They are 'F.C.' I expect you can guess what they stand for!

A Christmas Wish

A Christmas Wish

ONCE UPON a time there was a poor boy named Sam. He lived in the Far North in a little house made entirely of wood. He had four little sisters and four little brothers, all younger than he was. His father had died several years before, and Sam and his mother had to work very hard to get food for them all to eat.

They had worked hard all year and now it was nearly Christmas time. All the children were getting very excited. One day, they stopped to gaze at a brightly lit shop window.

'Look at the beautiful decorations!' cried Sam's youngest sister.

'Look at all the delicious food!' cried his twin brothers together.

'And, oh, look at all the lovely toys!' cried a third brother. 'Sam, shall we have toys and good things to eat this Christmas?'

'I don't know,' said Sam. 'They cost a lot of money, and it is as much as we can do to buy bread. But if I can buy you toys, then you know that I will.'

Sam didn't really think he would be able to buy his brothers and sisters what they wanted, even though it was his own heart's desire. His mother had been ill for many weeks and could not work, so they had not been able to save any money for Christmas presents. Sam doubted that they would even have enough to buy some special food for Christmas Day – a turkey, perhaps, or a plump plum-pudding. But he was a cheerful little boy and didn't give up hope, so out he went to work every day with a smile.

As he was walking along, Sam planned what

he would do if only he could save some money from his wages.

'I'd buy a beautiful scarf and some chocolates for Mother, and a toy each for the boys and girls,' he thought. 'And I'd buy some lovely food for all of us. How nice that would be!'

But Christmas came nearer and nearer, and still Sam had no money to buy anything. Try as he might, he couldn't seem to save even a penny and as the days ticked by he began to look worried.

At last Christmas Eve came, and Sam knew his little brothers and sisters would have to go without toys or turkey. He was very sad as he walked slowly home after his long day's work.

It was late and very dark, and the snow lay thick on the ground. Huge, feathery snowflakes fell softly against his cheeks, and he wrapped his coat more tightly round him, for it was cold.

He shivered as the snow seeped through his worn-out boots, making his feet feel like lumps of ice. Poor

Sam! This was surely the most dismal Christmas he had ever known.

Suddenly there came a sound of sleigh bells, and down the road glided a sleigh drawn by reindeer. It went past so quickly that Sam couldn't see who was driving it. But as the sleigh passed him, something dropped at his feet, blown there by the wind.

Sam picked it up and looked at it by the light of his lamp. It was made of soft red velvet, trimmed with white fur.

'It's a cap!' cried Sam. 'The driver of that sleigh must have lost it in the wind. I'll see if he comes back for it.'

But though Sam waited a long time, no one came, so at last he went home with the red cap in his pocket.

He was wet through with the snow, and his feet were frozen solid with the cold as he wiped his boots on the mat at home.

His youngest sister, Sarah, who had been tucked up in bed, ran to greet him with a hug and a kiss. The rest of the children were fast asleep.

'You must be freezing, Sam,' said his mother when she saw him. 'And look at your poor wet feet!'

'Yes,' said Sam, sighing. 'My boots are nearly worn out now. I wish I had a new pair!'

And whatever do you think! Just as he said that, his old boots flew out of the door, and a pair of brand-new ones flew in!

Sam stared in disbelief. His mother rubbed her eyes, and looked again and again – but it was true. There stood a pair of fine new boots.

'This is magic,' said Sam. 'But I wish you could have a pair of fine new boots as well, Mother dear!'

And almost before he had finished speaking, in flew another pair of boots which landed right next to the first! The two stared at them in amazement.

'Well, well!' said Sam's mother. 'This is certainly magic. But where is it coming from! Have you been speaking to pixies, my boy?'

'Oh no, Mother,' said Sam. Then he suddenly

remembered the red cap in his pocket, and he pulled it out. 'Maybe it has something to do with this,' he said, and told his mother how he had found it.

'It must be a wishing cap!' said Sam joyfully. 'Oh, Mother! We'll wish for toys and a turkey, shall we? And oh! I would like a nice warm fire to dry myself by!'

Immediately a great fire blazed up in the chimney, and Sam hurried over to it, laughing happily.

But his mother looked worried and took the soft velvet cap from his hands.

'Sam,' she said. 'This is someone else's wishing cap, not ours. The owner of it may be looking everywhere for it. We must give it back at once and not use it to wish for more things for ourselves.'

'But how do we find who it belongs to, Mother?' asked Sam.

'Well, you've only got to wish that the owner was here, and the wishing cap will bring him,' she replied, handing the cap back to her son.

Sam knew she was right. It would be wrong to keep a wishing cap belonging to someone else. So he wished once again.

'I wish the owner of this cap was here,' he said loudly.

And can you guess who, seconds later was standing there in front of them? Why, there in the middle of the floor, stood Santa Claus himself! Sam and his mother could hardly believe their eyes.

Santa looked very surprised at first, but when he saw his red velvet cap in Sam's hands, he understood what had happened.

'So you found my hat!' he said, and he broke into such a loud and jolly laugh that it brought all the younger children running from their beds. How surprised they were to find Santa standing there.

'This is a piece of luck!' said Santa, smiling. 'For I need my cap especially tonight. You see, when my sack of toys gets empty, I wish it full again!'

Sam stared at Santa Claus in delight. Fancy the

wishing cap belonging to him! He gave it back with a smile.

'I'm sorry to say we got two pairs of boots and this warm fire by using your cap,' said Sam. 'I hope it hasn't done the magic in it any harm.'

'Bless you, no!' laughed Santa. 'It was splendid of you to wish to find the owner. Lots of people wouldn't have done that. But if you'd kept my cap for yourself, you'd soon have found that it brought you bad luck and unhappiness, instead of good fortune and joy. Thank you very much for giving it back to me. Now I must be off. I have a hundred thousand homes to visit tonight!'

Off went the jolly man, tramping out into the snow, and then Sam heard the sound of sleigh bells going down the road.

Next morning you should have heard the shrieks and shouts and squeaks and squeals of joy in Sam's home! Everybody's stocking was full to the brim with the things they wanted most – and Sam had a huge pile of presents on his bed too.

His mother found a lovely red scarf and a purse full of money in her stocking – and when she went downstairs she gasped in surprise. On the table lay the biggest turkey she had ever seen, a monster plum-pudding and plates full of mince-pies!

'Thank you, Santa!' she whispered. All around them were apples and oranges, sweets and chocolates, and in the far corner was a Christmas tree, hung with more presents. And who do you think was on the top of the tree? Why, a little Santa Claus dressed in red, smiling at all the happy children.

'Wasn't it a good thing I found that wishing cap!' said Sam.

'And wasn't it a good thing you found the owner!' said his mother.

'Yes!' chorused the children, dancing up and down in excitement. 'Now we're going to have the best Christmas Day ever. Aren't we the luckiest family in the whole world?'

They all had a perfectly lovely Christmas after that, and when they were dancing round the tree in the evening, they suddenly heard a chuckling laugh. It sounded just like Santa Claus! But he wasn't anywhere in the room, and Sam thought it must have been the little Santa Claus stuck on the top of the tree.

I wonder if it was, don't you?

He Belonged
to the Family

He Belonged
to the Family

'YOU CLEAR away the tea for me, Janet,' said Mother. 'Daddy and I have something important to settle.'

Janet pricked up her ears. 'What is it, Mother? May I listen – or is it secret?'

'Oh no – it's not secret,' said her mother. 'But it's rather exciting. Daddy's going to buy a lorry!'

'A lorry!' said Janet. 'Whatever for?'

'To take round the logs, of course,' said Mother. 'Old Brownie's slow, now – and can only pull a small load of logs. Daddy wants to take three times as many out at a time, and so he thinks he'll buy a lorry.'

'Brownie will be pleased,' said Janet. 'He will have a nice rest in the field.'

'Oh, I shall sell him,' said Daddy, raising his head from the advertisements he was looking at.

Janet stared in horror. 'DADDY! Sell Brownie – our dear old horse! Why – I never remember a time without him. Daddy, you *can't* sell Brownie!'

'I've had a very good offer for him already,' said Daddy. 'From Mr Lucas, down at the farm.'

Janet stared at her father and mother as if she couldn't believe her ears. 'You *can't* sell old Brownie,' she said again, with tears in her eyes. 'Mother – he's one of the family. He really is. I love him. So does Paul.'

'Well, we're fond of him, too,' said her father. 'But we have to be sensible about things, Janet. *I* need a lorry – Mr Lucas will buy Brownie. It all fits nicely.'

'It doesn't, it doesn't,' cried Janet. 'You know

Mr Lucas is horrid. Oh, Daddy – I can't believe it. Does Paul know?'

Paul was her brother. He was out shutting up the hens, and having a word with Brownie in his old stable.

'No – Paul doesn't know yet,' said Mother. Janet put down the cups she was carrying and rushed to the door. 'I'm going to tell him,' she said. 'He'll beg and beg you not to sell dear old Brownie.'

The door slammed behind her. She ran out into the cold night. 'Paul! Paul! Where are you?'

'Here. With Brownie,' shouted Paul. In half a minute his sister was flying in at the stable door. She caught his arm.

'Paul! Did you know Daddy was buying a lorry – and selling Brownie to Mr Lucas?'

Paul whistled. 'No! He *can't* do that! Sell our Brownie! Why, he'd be absolutely *miserable*! He loves us.'

'Just at Christmas-time, too,' said Janet, sniffing

her tears away. 'Can't you *beg* Daddy not to do such a dreadful thing?'

Paul rubbed Brownie's velvety nose, and the horse nuzzled against him, pushing gently. He loved this boy and girl. The were always good to him, always kind. They had often ridden on him on the way to school when their father had taken his loaded cart of logs to deliver round the town. They were his friends.

Daddy wouldn't alter his mind. 'NO,' he said. 'And please don't be silly over this. I'm not going to turn down a good offer for Brownie. And I do want that lorry. In fact, I've ordered it. It can take three times as great a load as Brownie can pull.'

'Well, Daddy – after all the years of good work Brownie's done for you, I think it's *dreadful* to sell him to that horrid Mr Lucas,' said Paul. 'You could easily keep him to pull the little cart when you want it. You'll still use it for odd things.'

'Stop talking about it,' said Daddy getting cross.

'I've made up my mind – and when I do that I don't change it!'

So there was no more to be said! The lorry was to arrive after Christmas, and Brownie was to be walked down to Mr Lucas. It quite spoilt the excitement of Christmas week for the two children. They spent all their spare moments with Brownie. They rode to school on him every day, and when he came to the school gate he always stopped.

Then they slipped off his broad back, rubbed his nose, and watched him clip-clop away with the little cart loaded with logs behind him.

'You won't be able to ride on Brownie tomorrow when you go to school,' said their mother. 'Daddy is starting out later, hoping the snow will have melted a little. It's so hard for Brownie to pull the cart over that hard snow up the hill.'

'Oh dear – and it's our last day this term,' said Janet, disappointed. 'We break up tomorrow. After Christmas Brownie will be gone – and we shan't be able to ride him any more! I did so want to ride on him for the last time tomorrow.'

'You can catch the bus with *me*,' said her mother. 'I'm going Christmas shopping tomorrow, and I want to go early. We'll all catch the bus together, and leave Daddy to see himself off.'

So the next day Janet, Paul and their mother set off together to catch the bus. 'Mind how you go,' said Mother. 'It's terribly slippery today!'

So it was! They slithered and slipped down the path to the little front gate, and made their way carefully to the bus-stop. The bus came up and they all caught it. The children got out at the school gate and Mother went on to the shops in the bus.

At home their father finished looking through his order book, wrote a few letters, and then looked out of the window. The sun was out. Perhaps the hard snow up the hill would have melted. He would go out, load his cart, and get Brownie. So out he went, pulling on his thick overcoat.

Just outside the door he slipped and fell heavily. A dreadful pain shot through his right leg. He lay there groaning for a minute or two and then tried to pull himself up. But another pain came and he fell back.

'My leg must be broken,' he thought. 'What shall I do? There's no one in the house. My wife has gone off with the children and won't be back for hours. Nobody will hear me if I call.'

He was so cold and in such pain that he called as loudly as he could, though he knew there was no one to hear him. 'Help! Help!'

No one came. He called again. Then he stopped. What was the good of wasting his strength in shouting when he knew nobody could hear him?

But somebody had heard him! Old Brownie, up in his stable heard his master shouting. He raised his head. He was already puzzled because no one had come to fetch him and fasten him to the cart. He backed out of his stall and turned himself round to face the door. He knew quite well how to open it!

He nuzzled against the latch, trying to lift it with his mouth – and at last he did! He pushed the door. It swung open, and he went out into the snowy paddock.

He could see no one about. He went to the gap in the hedge and jumped through it. Then he trotted cautiously to the front gate of the little house where his master lived. He put his big brown head over the gate.

He saw his master lying on the ground! How astonishing! Brownie whinnied a little. The man looked up and saw him.

'Brownie! You got out by yourself – but you can't help me, old fellow!' he said, feebly.

Brownie pushed against the gate but it wouldn't open. He whinnied again, looking at his master. What could he do?

Then he turned and lumbered away up the road. His master groaned again. Even his horse had left him!

But old Brownie had had an idea. There was

something wrong with his master. His mistress wasn't there. The children had gone to school. He must fetch one of them.

He climbed the snowy hill, almost falling himself, it was so slippery. He came to the top and went along to the main road. He knew the way quite well. He would go to the school – that place where the children slid off his back each morning, and disappeared.

He came at last to the school gates. They were open. He went in and his great hooves made a muffled clip-clopping sound over the snowy playground. He stopped at the school door. It was shut.

He walked round the building and came to a window. He knew about windows. He had sometimes looked in them before, on his rounds with the cart. So he looked in this one now, but the room was empty.

He went on to the next window – and he looked in that one, his breath steaming the glass so that he couldn't very well see inside.

A class of children were at work in the room. Paul

and Janet were there. Paul looked up at the window – and he gave such a shout that everyone in the room jumped violently.

'LOOK! It's our old BROWNIE!' shouted Paul. He leapt up and went to the window. Janet ran too.

'He's by himself. He hasn't got the cart. He hasn't even a bridle on,' said Paul, in wonder. He opened the window and Brownie put his great head in. 'Why have you come, Brownie? Why aren't you with Daddy?'

'Hrrrrrumph!' said Brownie, wisely. Paul looked worried. 'Miss James – please may I go with Brownie? Something must have happened to my father. He should be with him.'

It wasn't long before Paul and Janet were up on Brownie's back, going as quickly as they dared over the slippery snow to their home. And there, on the front path, frozen cold and groaning in pain, they found their poor father!

They dragged him carefully indoors. Janet ran for the doctor. Paul got hot-water bottles and a hot drink for his father. Then the doctor came, and was soon busy setting the broken leg.

The children watched anxiously, helping in all they could – and somebody else watched too – old Brownie watched through the window, wondering what was happening! The doctor saw the big brown head there and smiled.

'That horse of yours is as concerned about you as much as the children are,' he told his patient. 'Did you hear that he actually walked all the way to their school, and fetched them back here to you to help you? Wonderful old fellow he must be.'

'He *is*,' said the children's father, turning his head to see Brownie's face at the window. 'He heard me calling and somehow got out of his stable to come to me. He put his head over the gate and saw I was in trouble – and off he went. I shall never, never part with old Brownie!'

Well! What do you think of *that?* The children cried out in delight.

'*Daddy!* Do you mean that? Aren't you going to get the lorry then?'

'Yes, of course – but I'm going to keep Brownie as well now. He'll run the cart around when your mother wants it for her shopping, and when she wants to take eggs and vegetables to the market. He shall be hers and yours. Can't sell him now, the faithful old friend!'

'Well – *now* Christmas will be lovely!' said Janet happily. 'I felt as if it was all spoilt. But it isn't. Dear old Brownie – shall I give him an extra big feed, Daddy?'

'Yes – all the oats he can eat!' said her father, smiling. 'And a special pat from me. Whatever made me think we could do without Brownie?'

So Christmas was very happy after all. The children had a beautiful Christmas tree, and after tea on Christmas day they lit all the candles on it.

Brownie came to see. They opened the window for him to put his big brown nose through. He stood there happily and watched the children playing round the tree. There was a present for him, of course!

'Here you are – a carrot from me and an apple from Paul!' said Janet and Brownie munched them hungrily. He belonged to the family. He was happy.

He *still* belongs. I know that because I see Janet and Paul riding him every Saturday!

A Hole in
Her Stocking

A Hole in
Her Stocking

MELANIE WAS ten years old, so she was a big girl. She was supposed to make her own bed, to dust her own room, to mend her clothes and to darn her stockings.

But Melanie was lazy. She often pulled her bed together instead of making it properly. She sometimes flicked the duster over her room instead of dusting every corner. She often used safety-pins to pin her dress together when a button was off, and if a hole in her stocking didn't show she wouldn't darn it!

Melanie lived with her aunt and her three cousins

in a country village. Her father and mother were away at work, and she had quite a nice time with her cousins. There was Oliver, the boy, and Jane and Gemma, the two girls. Melanie and the two girls slept together in a big bedroom that had three little beds in it.

Christmas-time was coming, and the children wondered what presents they would get. What fun to wake up on Christmas morning and see their stockings full! How lovely to see what was in them, right down to the toes!

When Christmas Eve came they could *not* go to sleep. Melanie's aunt saw them into bed and told them to hang up their longest stockings.

'And we'll hope they will be full in the morning,' she said.

Melanie looked in her drawer. She pulled out a long, black stocking. It had a big hole in the toe, but she hadn't bothered to mend it, because it didn't show when she wore her shoe on her foot. She took out the stocking and hung it at the head of the bed, twisting it round the knob.

'My stocking's ready!' she said.

'So are ours!' said the others. They all got into bed and tried to go to sleep. But they talked and laughed such a lot that it was quite impossible to sleep. Melanie's aunt came in at last and spoke quite sternly. 'If I hear one more word I shall take down your stockings and put them back into the drawer!'

After that there wasn't even a whisper. It would have been too dreadful to have no stockings on Christmas morning!

Now, that night all the stockings were filled. Shall I tell you what went into Melanie's stocking? Well, first of all, a bright one pound coin. It fell down the stocking – right to the toe – and, alas, because there was a hole there, it dropped out of the toe on to the carpet and rolled under the bed! The next thing put in was a dear little red ball – and that dropped out of the big hole and rolled away to a corner of the room!

Then a stick of barley-sugar, wrapped in bright paper, slipped into the stocking – and out of the toe! Next came a blue pencil and a little square rubber. Both of them dropped down to the toe – and out of the hole. They fell to the floor and bounced away.

Then a little red apple was put in – and that almost *did* stay in the stocking, for it was nearly as big as the hole. But it hung for a moment over the hole and then dropped with a soft bounce on to the floor, where it rolled off under the chest-of-drawers.

Then came a tiny doll, dressed like a sailor, and he fell out of the hole almost as soon as he was put in the stocking! Last of all there was a bar of chocolate, and that fell out, too. So, by the time that the other children's stockings were filled to the top, poor Melanie's was quite empty!

In the morning Jane awoke first. She gave a squeal at the sight of her bulging stocking and sat up at once. Gemma awoke and squealed, too.

'Melanie! Wake up! It's Christmas morning!' cried

Gemma. 'Our stockings are full. Oh, I've got *such* a dear little doll!'

'And I've got a duck to float in the bath!' said Jane. There was a yell from the other room.

'Hey, you girls! Come and look what I've got! I've got a clown who turns head-over-heels!'

This sounded so exciting that Jane and Gemma picked up their stockings and rushed into Oliver's room to see his clown.

Melanie sat up, excited. She looked at the stocking at the head of her bed. It didn't look very fat. She put out her hand to feel it. It didn't *feel* fat, either! She pulled it towards her. She put her hand in – right the way down – and there was nothing, nothing, nothing in it at all!

The little girl's heart sank. Why was there nothing in it? What had happened? Was there a present on her bed, perhaps? No, there was nothing there either. There was no present from anyone.

'They don't like me,' she thought, and tears came

into her eyes. 'They don't think I'm a nice little girl. No one has given me anything!'

She dressed quickly and slipped downstairs. She hid behind the big curtains at the sitting-room window.

'Where's Melanie?' asked Jane, in a surprised voice, when everyone was sitting at breakfast. 'I haven't seen her since we went into Oliver's room this morning.'

'There she is – behind the curtain!' said Oliver suddenly. 'She's crying! Melanie, what's the matter?'

'There was n-n-n-nothing in my st-st-stocking!' wept Melanie. 'I hadn't any presents at all. Nobody loves me!'

'But, darling, of course we all love you!' said her aunt in surprise. 'You've made a mistake, Melanie – your stocking is full! I expect you took the wrong stocking! Go upstairs and get it. Bring it down here and you'll see how full it is!'

Melanie went upstairs. She took the empty stocking and sadly brought it down to show everyone. Oliver put his hand right down to the toe – and his fingers came waggling out of the end!

He gave a shout of laughter. 'Melanie! You chose a stocking with a big, big hole in it, you silly! You chose one you put away without darning, naughty girl! All your presents must have dropped out! They will be on the floor!'

Everyone rushed upstairs to look – and, sure enough, there was the one pound coin on the floor under the bed – and there was the ball – and the barley-sugar – and the doll – and the chocolate – and everything. All on the floor. Melanie didn't know whether to laugh or to cry.

'Oh dear!' she said. 'Oh dear! How silly I am! And, oh, I do feel ashamed of that big hole I didn't darn! Oh, Auntie, I'm so sorry. I know I should mend holes in my stockings – and haven't I been well punished for forgetting!'

'Never mind, dear,' said her aunt. 'Everything is all right now. You've got a lovely lot of presents and

Christmas is going to be great!'

So it was – and I expect you know what one of Melanie's New Year Resolutions was, don't you? Yes – to be sure and darn every hole in her stockings.

Christmas in
the Toyshop

Christmas in
the Toyshop

ONCE UPON a time there was a toyshop. It sold sweets as well as toys, so it was a very nice shop indeed.

All the children loved it. They used to come each day and press their noses against the window, and look in to see what toys there were.

'Oh, look at that beautiful doll!' they would say. 'Oh, do you see that train with its three carriages – and it's got lines to run on too.'

'Look at the rocking-horse. I do love his friendly face!'

'Oh, what a lovely shop this is! When we grow up let's keep a shop just like this one!'

Miss Roundy, the shopkeeper, liked having a toyshop. She liked seeing the children and showing them all her toys, and she nearly always gave them an extra sweet or two in their bags when they came to spend their pocket money. So, of course, the children all loved her.

The toys loved her, too.

'Look – she found me a new key when mine dropped behind the shelf and couldn't be found,' said the clockwork train.

'And she put a spot of red paint on my coat where some got rubbed off,' said one of the toy soldiers. 'She's very, very kind.'

The toys liked living in Miss Roundy's shop till they were bought by the children. It was fun to sit on the shelves and the counter, and watch the boys and girls come in and hear them talk. And it was very exciting when one of them was bought, and taken proudly away by a child.

The toys didn't like Sundays as much as weekdays, because then the shop was shut, and nobody came to see them at all. They couldn't bear it when Miss Roundy took her summer holiday and shut the shop for a whole fortnight! That was dreadful.

'It's so dull,' complained the biggest teddy bear, and he pressed his middle to make himself growl mournfully. 'There's no one to see and nothing to do. Miss Roundy even pulls down the window-blind so that we can't see the children looking in at us.'

And then Christmas time came, and the toys had a shock. Miss Roundy was going to close the shop for four whole days and go away to stay with her aunt. Oh dear!

'Four days of dullness and quietness and darkness,' said the rocking-horse, gloomily. 'Nothing to do. No one to come and buy us, or see how nice we are. Four whole days!'

A black monkey with a red ribbon round his neck

spoke in a high, chattering voice. 'Can't we have a Christmas party for ourselves?'

'It's an idea,' said the rocking-horse, smiling. 'Let's all think about it till Christmas comes – then we'll have a grand time in here by ourselves!'

The day came when Miss Roundy was going to shut the shop. She pulled down the big window-blind. Then she turned to the watching toys.

'I'm going now, toys,' she said. 'I shan't see you again for four whole days. Be good. A happy Christmas to you – and try and have a good time yourselves. Do what you like – I shan't mind! Happy Christmas!'

She went out of the shop and locked the door. The toys heard her footsteps going down the street.

'Happy Christmas, Miss Roundy!' said everyone, softly. 'You're nice!'

And now they were all alone for four days. What were they going to do?

The toys did what they always did as soon as the shop was shut for the night. They got up and stretched themselves, because they got stiff with sitting so long on the shelves and counter.

'That's better,' said the rag-doll, shaking out her legs one after another to loosen them.

The pink cat rolled over and over. 'Ah – that was good,' she said, standing up again. 'I do love a roll.'

The little clockwork train whistled loudly and the toy soldiers climbed out of their boxes and began marching to and fro. 'Nice to stretch our legs a bit,' they said, and then they scattered because the roly-poly man came rolling along, not looking where he was going, as usual.

'Look out,' cried the captain of the soldiers, 'you'll bump into the doll's-house! There he goes, rolling to and fro – what a way to get about!'

'Listen, everyone!' called the rocking-horse. 'Let's talk about Christmas.'

'When is it?' asked the big teddy bear.

'The day after tomorrow,' said the rocking-horse. 'I think if we're going to have a good Christmas ourselves we ought to make our plans now, and get everything going, so that we're ready by Christmas Day.'

'Oh yes!' cried everyone, and they all came round the rocking-horse. What a crowd there was. All the little doll's-house dolls, and the other bigger dolls, the skittles, the railway train with its carriages, and another wooden train, and the roly-poly man, and – well, I couldn't possibly tell you them all, but you know what toys there are in a toyshop, don't you?

'Sit down,' said the rocking-horse. And everyone sat, except, of course the things that could only stand, like the trains and the motor-cars and the balls.

'We shall want a party,' said the rocking-horse. 'That means we must have things to eat. We can take any of the sweets and chocolates we like, to make into cakes and things – Miss Roundy said we were to help ourselves.'

'We can make the food,' said the doll's-house dolls.

'We'll help,' said the skittles, excitedly.

'We can cook on that nice toy stove over there,' said the twin dolls. One of the twins was a boy doll and the other was a girl doll, and they were exactly alike.

'I think the pink cat and the black monkey could arrange a circus,' said the rocking-horse. 'They'll have great fun working together on that.'

'I'll do the Christmas tree,' said the sailor doll. 'We'll have presents for everyone under it! We'll play games afterwards, too.'

'What a pity Father Christmas doesn't know about us!' said the roly-poly man. 'It would be so nice if he came to the party.'

'I don't suppose he'll be able to come,' said the black monkey. 'He's much too busy at Christmas time. Don't roll against me like that, Roly-Poly Man. You'll knock me over.'

The roly-poly man rolled away and bumped into a row of soldiers. They went down on the floor at once. As they got up and brushed themselves down, they shouted angrily at the roly-poly man.

'Don't let's quarrel,' said the rocking-horse. 'People should never quarrel at Christmas time. It's a time to make one another happy and glad. Now – to your work, everyone – and we'll see what a wonderful Christmas Day we will have!'

The dolls and the skittles set to work at once. The doll with golden hair and the twin dolls took charge of the cooking. They got the little toy cooker going, and there was soon a most delicious smell in the toyshop – the cakes were baking!

There were chocolate cakes and fudge cakes and peppermint buns. There were little jellies made of the jelly sweets Miss Roundy sold. There was a very big iced cake, with tiny candles on it that the rag-doll had found in a box.

The baking and cooking went on all day long. The twin dolls had to scold the roly-poly man ever so many times because he would keep rolling against the golden haired doll just as she was taking cakes out of the oven.

Still, as you can see, there was plenty of everything.

'What a feast we are going to have!' said the rag-doll, greedily. 'Oooh – fudge cakes – I'll have six of those, please, on Christmas Day!'

The sailor doll did the Christmas tree. He was very, very clever. He climbed right up to the topmost shelf, which Miss Roundy had decorated with evergreens, and he chose a very nice bit of fir.

'Look out!' he called. 'I'm going to push it off the shelf.' So everyone looked out, and down came the little branch of fir-tree, flopping on to the floor.

The sailor doll climbed down. He did a little dance of joy when he saw what a wonderful tree the bit of fir would make. He wondered what to put it in.

'If you'll get me out of my box, so that I can join in the fun for once, you can use my box,' said the gruff voice of Jack-in-the-box.

The toys didn't really like Jack-in-the-box very much. He lived inside a square box, and when the box was opened he suddenly leaped out on a long spring, and frightened them very much. The sailor doll didn't really know if he wanted to get Jack out of his box.

'Go on – just this once,' said Jack-in-the-box. 'I promise to be good. I'll perform in the circus, and be funny if you like.'

So Jack-in-the-box was taken out of his box and he wobbled everywhere on his long spring, enjoying his freedom very much.

The box was just right for the Christmas tree. The sailor doll filled it with earth that he took from the pot that held a big plant belonging to Miss Roundy. Then he planted the bit of fir-tree in it.

'Now to decorate it!' he said. So he got some tiny coloured candles and some bright beads out of the bead-box, and some tinsel from the counter, and anything else he could think of – and dear me, the tree really began to look very beautiful!

'I can make a star to go on the top of the tree,' said the teddy bear, and he ran off to find some silver paper.

'And now you're none of you to look,' said the

sailor, 'because I'm going to pack up presents for you – yes, a present for every single one of you!'

The circus was practising hard. There were two clockwork clowns in the toyshop, so they were exactly right for the circus. They could go head over heels as fast as could be.

'We want some horses,' said the black monkey, who was very busy. 'Pink cat, stop prowling round the cakes, and see how many horses you can find.'

The roly-poly man said he wanted to be a clown, so the teddy bear made him a clown's hat, and let him roll about the ring, knocking people over. Jack-out-of-his-box jumped about and waggled his head on his long neck. He was really very funny.

The pink cat borrowed some horses from the soldiers and the farm. She led them down to the circus ring.

Noah arrived with his animals from the ark. There were elephants, lions, tigers and even kangaroos!

'It's going to be a grand circus!' said the pink cat. 'Oh, hurry up and come, Christmas Day!'

Well, Christmas Day did come at last! The toys rushed to one another, shouting 'Happy Christmas! Happy Christmas!' at the tops of their voices.

The railway train whistled its loudest. The big bear and the little bears pressed themselves in the middle and growled. The musical box began to play, and the rag-doll sat down at the toy piano and played a jolly tune.

Nobody knew she could play and they were all very surprised. So was the ragdoll. She hadn't known either and once she had begun to play she couldn't stop! So what with the engine's whistle, the bears' growling, the musical box's tunes and the piano there was a splendid noise!

The roly-poly man got so excited that he knocked over two of the horses, rolled on the monkey's tail and upset a jug of lemonade.

'Can't you stop rolling about and be still for a moment?' said the pink cat, keeping her tail well out of the way.

'I can't stand still,' said the roly-poly man, 'because I've got something very heavy at the bottom of me. It makes me wobble, but not fall over. I really will try to be good – but if you were as wobbly as I am you'd find it difficult, too.'

The black monkey suddenly appeared dressed up in white trousers and a top hat! He carried a whip in his hand. He cracked it and made everyone jump.

Then the pink cat appeared, carrying a drum. She beat it – *boom-diddy-boom-boom-boom.*

'The circus is about to begin!' shouted the black monkey and he cracked his whip again. 'Walk up, everyone! The circus is about to begin!'

Boom-diddy-boom-diddy-boom! went the drum.

All the toys rushed for seats. The black monkey had arranged bricks of all sizes and shapes out of the brick-boxes for seats and there was room for everyone. The doll's-house dolls were allowed to be at the front because they were so small.

The skittles were so excited that they kept giggling and falling over.

'Quiet there! Settle down, please!' shouted the monkey. 'Pink cat, sound the drum again – the performers are about to march in.'

The circus began. You really should have seen it. The horses were splendid. They ran round the ring one way, and then turned and went the other way.

Then the clowns came on, with Jack and the roly-poly man. The roly-poly man rolled all over the place and knocked all the clowns over. Then the clowns tried to catch Jack, but they couldn't, of course, because Jack sprang about all over the place, on his long spring. The toys almost cried with laughter.

The elephants were cheered when they came in. They waved their trunks in the air and trumpeted as loudly as they could. The lions and tigers came in and roared fiercely. The kangaroos jumped all round the ring and the bears walked in, standing up on their hind legs.

All the toys clapped and cheered and stamped at the end, and said it was the very best circus in the world.

The pink cat and the black monkey felt very proud and they stood in the middle of the ring and bowed to everyone so many times that they really made their backs ache.

'Now for the tea party!' called the doll with golden hair. 'Come along! You must be very hungry, toys – hurry up and come to the party!'

What a wonderful tea party it was! There were little tables everywhere. In the middle of them were vases of flowers that the dolls had picked out of the dolls' hats that Miss Roundy kept in a box on a special shelf.

The tables were set with the cups and saucers and plates out of the boxes of toy tea sets. There was a teapot on each, full of lemonade to pour into the cups.

The cakes were lovely. There were fudge cakes, peppermint buns, chocolate cakes, all kinds of biscuits, toffee sandwiches, jellies that wobbled like the roly-poly man and, of course, the Christmas cake with its candles was the best thing of all.

'We've put it on a table by itself, because it's so big,' said the golden-haired doll. 'I hope there'll be a slice for everybody.'

It looked lovely. The rag-doll had decorated it with icing. Everyone thought that was very clever indeed.

The pink cat ate so much that she got fatter than ever. The captain of the soldiers lent the twin dolls his sharp sword to cut the cake. The roly-poly man rolled up to see them cutting it, and nearly got his head cut off!

When nobody could eat any more, and all the lemonade was drunk, the skittles cleared away. 'We'll do the washing-up and put all the tea sets back in their boxes,' they said. 'The rest of you can play games.'

So, while the skittles were busy, the toys played party games. They played blindman's-buff, and the blindfolded pink cat caught the elephant out of the Noah's ark.

'Who can it be?' wondered the pink cat, feeling the elephant carefully. All the toys laughed, because of course, they knew who it was.

They played hunt the thimble, and nobody could see for a long time where the thimble was hidden. Then the sailor doll gave a scream.

'The captain of the soldiers is wearing it for a helmet – he is, he is!'

And so he was. He was sorry to give it up because he thought it was a very nice helmet indeed.

The train gave everyone rides, and so did the toy motor-cars. Even the aeroplane said it would fly round the room once with everybody. The musical box played hard for anyone who wanted to dance.

The roly-poly man made everyone laugh when he tried to dance with the rag-doll. He rolled about so much that he knocked everyone off the floor.

They were all having such a good time. Then

suddenly they noticed that all the candles on the Christmas tree were alight!

'Oh, oh! It's time for the Christmas tree!' cried the toys, and they rushed over to it. 'Isn't it pretty? Look at the star at the top!'

'Where's the sailor doll?' said the roly-poly man.

'Gone to fetch Father Christmas, he told me,' said the rocking-horse. 'Do you suppose he meant it?'

And then, would you believe it, there came the noise of bells!

'Sleigh bells! It really is Father Christmas coming!' cried all the toys, and they rushed to the chimney. 'He's coming! He's coming!'

Down the chimney came a pair of boots – then a pair of red trousers – and then with a jump, down on the rug came a merry, white-whiskered fellow, whose red hood framed his jolly red face.

'Father Christmas! You've come, you've come!' shouted the toys, and they dragged him to the tree.

'Wait a bit – I want my sack. It's just a little way up

the chimney,' said Father Christmas. So the big teddy bear fetched it. It was a nice big bumpy-looking sack.

'Happy Christmas, toys,' said Father Christmas. He was a very nice little Father Christmas, not much bigger than the dolls. The toys were glad. They would have been rather afraid of a great big one.

'Happy Christmas!' sang out everyone. Then Father Christmas undid his sack. Oh, what a lot of things he had! There were ribbons and brooches for the dolls, sweets for the soldiers, chocolates for the Noah's ark animals, and balls, made of red holly berries, for the toy animals. Nobody had been forgotten. It was wonderful.

Father Christmas handed out all the presents, beaming happily. Then he took a few presents from under the tree.

'These are special presents for the people who tried to make your Christmas so nice,' he said. 'Presents for the golden-haired doll and the twin dolls – and for the black monkey and the pink cat – here you are, special little presents for being kind and good.'

'But what about the sailor doll?' said the rocking-horse, at once. 'He did the tree, you know. Have you forgotten him?'

'Where is he?' said Father Christmas.

Well, dear me, he wasn't there! Would you believe it?

'I saw him last,' said the rocking-horse. 'He said he was going to fetch you, Father Christmas. Didn't he fetch you?'

'Well, I'm here, aren't I?' said Father Christmas, and he laughed. 'Dear me – it's sad there's no present for the sailor doll, but I don't expect he'll mind at all.'

The toys had opened all their presents. Somewhere a clock struck twelve. Midnight! Oh dear, how dreadfully late!

The twin dolls yawned loudly, and that made everyone yawn, too.

'We'd better clear up and go to bed,' said the golden-haired doll. 'Or we shall fall asleep on our feet, and that would never do.'

So they cleared up, and in the middle of it all Father Christmas disappeared. Nobody saw him go. The pink cat said she saw him go into the doll's-house, but he wasn't there when she looked.

Somebody else was, though – the sailor doll! The pink cat dragged him out.

'Here's the sailor doll!' she cried. 'Here he is! Sailor, you missed Father Christmas – oh, what a terrible pity!'

But, you know, he didn't! He was there all the time. Have you guessed? He was Father Christmas, of course, all dressed up. He had climbed up the chimney when nobody was looking. Wasn't he clever?

'You were Father Christmas!' cried the golden-haired doll, and she hugged him hard. 'You're a dear!'

'Yes, you are,' shouted the rocking-horse. 'That was the best part of all, when Father Christmas came. We were so sad there was no present for you. But you shall have one – you shall, you shall!'

And he did. The toys threaded a whole lot of red holly berries together, and made him the finest necklace he had ever had. I wish you could see him wearing it. He does look pleased.

Miss Roundy will never guess all that the toys did in her toyshop that Christmas Day, will she? If you ever meet her, you can tell her. I do wish I'd been there to see it all, don't you?

They Didn't Believe
in Santa Claus!

They Didn't Believe in Santa Claus!

'NOW, IS EVERYTHING ready?' called Santa Claus, as he sat in his sleigh on Christmas Eve, holding the reins of his four reindeer. 'Is my sack quite full? Have I got my notebook with the children's names and addresses in?'

'Yes. You've got everything, sir,' said his servant. 'Better go now, or you'll be late. The reindeer have just had a good meal and they'll be able to gallop well.'

So off went Santa Claus through the night! The reindeer galloped through the frosty air, high above the towns and villages, their bells jingling as they went. 'I've lost count of how many times I've been out like this on Christmas Eve now,' said Santa Claus to himself. 'Is it one thousand or eleven hundred – or even more? I just can't remember.'

He leaned down and looked at the town he was passing over. 'The things they have now that they didn't have in years gone by!' he said. 'Aeroplanes for instance – and those funny H-shaped things on the roofs of some of the houses – what do they call them – television masts!'

The reindeer galloped on, high above the roofs. Santa Claus looked at his list. He pulled at the reins as they came to a village. 'First call here,' he said. 'Let's see now – Gladys Hills and Sheila Pratt, Bobby and Jean MacDonald. All good children who deserve to have their stockings full from top to toe.'

The reindeer landed gently on the roof of a house, just by a chimney. In a trice Santa Claus had disappeared down the chimney. One of the reindeer put his nose down to see where he had gone. The soot made him sneeze. He was a young one, pulling the sleigh for the first time that Christmas.

They soon left that village and went to another, and then on to a town. And here the accident happened.

A Princess had come to visit the town the day before, and a tall flag-mast had been put up, with a flag right at the top. The flag still flew there, flapping in the wind.

Now the young, new reindeer didn't know what a flag was, and when he saw this flapping thing high up in the air, he was terrified. He reared up and almost upset the sleigh.

'Now, now!' cried Santa, crossly. 'Behave yourself, there!'

But the flag flapped again, and that was too much for the reindeer. He reared again, and then pulled away to the left, galloping with all his might, dragging the other three with him.

Alas! When the sleigh tipped up for the second

time, Santa Claus fell out. His sack didn't, though. Somehow or other that stayed safely on the sleigh. The reindeer disappeared into the night, leaving Santa Claus on the roof of a cottage. He hadn't had far to fall, luckily. He sat there, getting his breath.

'Here's a thing to happen!' he said, crossly. He wondered what to do. He felt for his whistle to whistle his reindeer back, but that had fallen off somewhere.

'Well, I must get down the chimney and ask for help,' thought Santa, and down the chimney he went.

It was a long chimney and landed him in a cold, empty dark room. He stepped out on to a hearthrug and at that very moment somebody switched on a light.

An old man stood at the door, and behind stood a fierce-looking old woman. The man held a poker, and he came into the room holding it as if he was going to hit Santa Claus.

'Hey, don't do that,' said Santa, in alarm. 'Don't you know me? I'm Santa Claus.'

The old man snorted rudely. 'What will you burglars think of next?' he said. 'Dressing up like that and coming down chimneys! *I* know what you've come for – to steal our silver.'

'Look here – I really am Santa Claus,' said Santa. 'Don't you believe me?'

'No. As if we believe in Santa Claus at our age!' said the old woman. 'In fact – I don't believe I *ever* did!'

'Oh, you naughty story-teller,' said Santa. 'Just let me remember now – weren't you once a little girl called Sarah Jane? And didn't I bring you a doll with black hair, blue eyes and a dress with pink roses all over it?'

'My name *is* Sarah Jane,' said the old woman, looking surprised. 'And, yes – I do remember the doll. But *you* didn't bring it – my mother must have given it to me.'

'And isn't this your brother?' went on Santa. 'Let me see – as far as I remember he wasn't a very nice little boy. His name was Peter John – and I brought him a toy boat called Lucy-Ann and a book called *Eyes and No-Eyes*. Yes, I remember that clearly. Years and years ago it was.'

The old man lowered the poker and stared in surprise. 'I don't know how you know all this,' he said. 'It's true my name is Peter John and I did have those things when I was a small boy – but it's no good trying to deceive *me*! You're no more Santa Claus than I am! You're a burglar wearing a silly disguise! And what's more I'm going to call the police!'

'Do,' said Santa Claus, sitting down in a chair. 'I shall probably know the policeman too. Do hurry up, though. I simply *must* get my reindeer back, and time's getting short. I've lots to do tonight.'

'Go and telephone, Sarah Jane,' said the old man to his sister, and she went into the hall. It wasn't long before a knocking came at the door, and two policemen walked in, one middle-aged and plump, the other young and shy.

'Arrest this fellow,' said the old man. 'He broke

into my house down the chimney dressed up as Santa Claus. Pretends to know all about us – the fraud!'

Santa Claus got up and held out his hand to the plump, middle-aged policeman. 'Why, if it isn't Harry Jones,' he said. 'Harry, you were one of the top children on my list forty years ago – best boy in the village, and I was to bring you a railway train with a tunnel and signal. I did, too – with a station thrown in because I was pleased to hear about you!'

The burly policeman gaped. His eyes almost fell out of his head. 'Sir,' he said, 'sir! My, I haven't believed in you for years! Oh, that railway set! I never had such a wonderful Christmas in my life as I had when I got that railway. I wrote you a letter of thanks, sir.'

'I got it,' said Santa Claus. 'Nicely written, too. And I know this young fellow here as well – why, it can't be more than twelve years ago since I took him a meccano set and a set of garden tools!'

'Seventeen years, sir,' said the young policeman,

grinning all over his face. 'Nicest presents I ever had, sir. I made my garden look lovely with those tools. I've still got the fork, sir.'

'You know, I had a letter this Christmas from a small boy called Bobby Brown,' said Santa Claus, fishing in his enormous pocket. 'You're called Bobby Brown, too, aren't you? Any relation?'

'Yes, sir. He's my little boy,' said the big Bobby Brown, blushing red with delight. 'What did he ask you for, sir?'

'An aeroplane and a box of chalks,' said Santa Claus, reading the letter. 'I had them in my sack for him, too. Now, goodness knows if I'll be able to fill any stockings tonight, with my reindeer gone off in a fright!'

The old man was listening to all this in a fine rage. He rapped the poker on the table. 'Police, do your duty. Surely *you* aren't taken in by this fellow. *You* don't believe in Santa Claus, do you?'

'Well – I didn't till I met him – not since I was a

kid,' said Bobby Brown. 'But how can I help knowing it *is* Santa Claus, sir? He did bring us those things when we were children. We can't arrest him. We can only help him.'

'Fine, fine,' said Santa. 'Have you got a police-whistle on you? I've dropped my reindeer whistle – but I daresay yours would do as well.'

'Here, sir,' said the young policeman eagerly, and he handed Santa Claus his whistle. Santa went to the window, opened it and blew three long blasts on the whistle and seven short ones. And in no time at all the five watchers saw a shadow in the eastern sky and heard the sound of bells. The four reindeer landed on the roof and waited for their master.

He disappeared up the chimney. 'Thank you,' he said to the policemen. 'So glad you still believe in me. Sarah Jane and Peter John don't, though, poor things!'

They didn't! Even though they had seen and heard him, they still didn't believe it was Santa Claus. What a pity!

Little Bobby Brown got his aeroplane and his chalks – and, will you believe it, the two policemen each got a little present, too – a tiny figure of Santa Claus to put on top of their Christmas cakes. They *were* pleased!

I hope nothing happens to Santa Claus this Christmas – but if it does and he comes into *your* house, help him, won't you! He really is the jolliest, kindest old fellow anyone can meet.

Bobbo's Magic Stocking

Bobbo's Magic Stocking

ONCE UPON a time, many years ago, there was a little boy called Bobbo. He lived with his father and mother in a nice house in London, and he had plenty of toys and plenty of pets.

In the house he had his puppy, Jock, and his kitten, Snowball, and two yellow canaries. In the garden he had two pet rabbits, and a chicken that laid him a brown egg every morning as regular as clockwork.

In the nursery was a tall rocking-horse and a bookcase with twenty books of adventure and fairy tales in it. In the toy cupboard were balls, railway trains, bricks, teddy bears, clowns, a box of paints, and a cricket bat. So you wouldn't think that Bobbo wanted anything else at all, would you?

But he did! He was always wanting something new. He was always tired of what he had got.

'Mummy, buy me this,' he would say; or, 'Daddy, buy me that!'

'You've got quite enough things,' said his parents, but more often than not they were foolish enough to buy Bobbo what he wanted, so that his toy cupboard was full almost to bursting.

The worst of it was that Bobbo would never give any of his toys away unless he was made to. He was a selfish little boy, who couldn't really be bothered to think about anybody else.

'I don't know how to cure him,' said his mother with a sigh.

'And I don't know how to cure him,' said his father with a frown.

But he *was* cured, and you will soon see how.

It happened that one night, about a week before Christmas Day, Bobbo was in bed, and couldn't get to sleep. He tried and he tried, but it was no use. He heard the clock in the hall strike nine, and ten, and then he heard his father and mother come up to bed. After a long time the clock struck eleven, and Bobbo knew that in an hour's time it would be midnight.

Fairies and elves come out at midnight, he thought to himself. I've never been awake at twelve o'clock before, so perhaps I may see or hear something surprising. I'll listen.

He lay in bed and listened to the sounds of the night. He heard the wind come whistling in at his window, and an owl hoot loudly. Then he heard another sound, a curious one that made him sit up, feeling puzzled.

It was the sound of sleigh bells, jingling in the distance! Nearer they came and nearer, and Bobbo jumped out of bed and ran to the window. It was a bright moonlit night, and he could see quite well down the snowy street. First of all, in the distance, he saw something coming along that looked like a carriage drawn by horses. And then he saw what it really was!

It was Santa Claus's sleigh, drawn by four fine reindeer with great branching antlers! The bells on the reins jingled loudly, but the reindeer themselves made no noise as they trotted along in the deep snow. Driving them was a large elf, and at the back, in the big sleigh, was a crowd of laughing children, all in their nightclothes, the boys in pyjamas and the girls in their frilly nightdresses.

Bobbo stared in astonishment. The sleigh came nearer and nearer, and then, just outside Bobbo's gate, it stopped. The elf threw the reins on to the backs of the reindeer, and then took up a big book and opened it. He ran his finger down a page, and then nodded his head as if he had found what he wanted.

He stepped down from the sleigh, and ran through

the gate of the house next to Bobbo's.

Oh, he's gone to fetch Nancy from next door, thought Bobbo. I suppose he's fetching all the children who have been extra good, to take them for a trip to Fairyland, or somewhere. Well, I'm sure he won't fetch me, because I know I haven't been good for quite a week. Still, I don't see why I shouldn't go and have a look at that sleigh. I'm quite certain it's the one that Santa Claus uses and I don't expect I'll ever get another chance of seeing it so close.

He put on his slippers, and ran down the stairs. He slipped the bolts of the front door, and then opened it. Out he went into the moonlight, feeling not in the least cold, for it was fairy weather that night.

Bobbo saw that the elf had not yet come back from the house next door, so he ran down the path to his front gate. He saw that the sleigh was a very big one, and that the reindeer were the loveliest he had ever seen.

As he ran up, the children in the sleigh leaned

out and saw him. They waved happily to him, and called him.

'Come along,' they said. 'Have you been a good boy, too?'

Bobbo stopped and looked at the children in the sleigh. He saw that they thought he was one of the good children that the elf was fetching. Quick as a flash Bobbo made up his mind to let them go on thinking so, for he thought that perhaps he would be able to go with them on the trip, if the elf did not see that he was an extra child.

He nodded and laughed to the children, and they put out their hands to him, and pulled him into the sleigh with them.

'Isn't it fun?' they said. 'Isn't it fun?'

'Where are we going?' asked Bobbo.

'Oh, don't you know?' said a golden-haired boy. 'We're going to visit the place where Santa Claus lives, and see all the toys being made! He always sends his elf to fetch good children every year, and this year it's *our* turn!'

'Here comes the elf!' cried a little girl. 'He's got a dear little smiling girl with him! Make room for her!'

All the children squashed up to make room for Nancy. Bobbo got right at the back of the sleigh, for he didn't want the elf to see him, and he felt sure that if Nancy spied him, she might make some remark about him. Nancy sat down in the front, and began to talk to all the children in an excited little voice.

'Now we're off again!' cried the elf, climbing into the driving-seat. 'Hold tight!'

He jerked the reins, and the reindeer started off again over the snow, pulling the sleigh so smoothly that Bobbo felt as if he was in a dream. Now that he really was off with the children he felt a little bit uncomfortable, for he didn't know what the elf might say when he found that he had one boy too many.

The sleigh went on and on and on, through the town and into the country. At last it stopped again before a tiny little cottage, and once more the elf looked up his address book, and found the names he wanted.

'There are two children to come from here,' he said, 'and then that's all. After we've got them, we'll go straight off to the home of Santa Claus, and see all the wonderful things he has to show you!'

He went through the gate and tapped softly at the door of the cottage. It was opened at once, and Bobbo saw two excited children standing there, one a girl and one a boy.

'Come on, twins,' said the elf, cheerfully. 'The sleigh is waiting.'

The two children ran to the sleigh, and jumped in. The elf once more took up the reins, and the sleigh began to move very quickly over the snow.

'Hold on as tightly as you can!' said the elf. 'I'm going to go at top speed, for we're a little late!'

All the children held on to each other and gasped in delight as the sleigh tore along over the snow at a most tremendous rate. The wind whistled by, and blew their hair straight out behind them, so that they laughed to see each other.

'Look at that hill!' the golden-haired boy cried suddenly. 'It's like a cliff, it's so steep!'

Bobbo looked, and he saw a most enormous hill stretching up in front of the sleigh. It was very, very steep, but the reindeer leapt up it as easily as if it was level ground. The sleigh tilted backwards, and the children held on more tightly than ever. Up and up went the sleigh, right to the very, very top, and then, on the summit, drenched in moonlight, it stopped.

'We've come to a little inn!' cried one of the children, leaning out. 'Oh, and here come six little gnomes, carrying something! What *are* they going to do?'

All the children leaned out to watch. They saw the gnomes come hurrying up, carrying pairs of lovely green wings. There were six pairs of these, and the gnomes knew just what to do with them.

Four of the gnomes went to the reindeer, and fastened a pair of wings on to their backs. The other two bent down by the sleigh, and the children saw that they had fastened two pairs of wings on to the sides of the sleigh as well!

'We're going to fly, we're going to fly!' they cried. 'Oh, what fun it will be!'

When the wings were all tightly fastened the gnomes stepped back. The elf driver gathered up the reins once more, and the reindeer plunged forward.

Bobbo looked all round. He could see a long, long way from the top of the steep hill, and the world looked very lovely in the silver moonlight. As the sleigh started forward again he saw that, instead of going down the other side of the hill, they had jumped straight off it, and were now galloping steadily through the air!

'My word!' thought Bobbo. 'Now we're off to Santa Claus's home! I do wonder what it will be like.'

The sleigh went on and on for a very long time, but the children didn't get at all tired, for they loved looking downwards and seeing the towns, villages, lakes, and seas they passed over. The elf answered their questions, and told them all they wanted to know.

'Do you see that great mountain sticking up into the sky?' he said at last. 'Well, that is where Santa Claus lives. In five minutes we shall be there.'

Bobbo began to wonder if he would be found out by Santa Claus when he arrived.

'Perhaps he won't notice,' he thought. 'There are so many children in the sleigh that surely he won't see there is one too many!'

Nearer and nearer to the mountain glided the sleigh, and at last it touched the summit. The reindeer felt their feet on firm ground once more, and the children shouted in delight.

On top of the mountain was built an enormous castle, its towers shining against the moonlit sky. Just as the sleigh bumped gently down to the ground, a big jolly man came running out of the great open door of the castle. He was dressed in red, and had big boots on and a pointed red hat.

'Santa Claus! Santa Claus!' cried all the children, and they scrambled out of the sleigh, and rushed to meet him as fast as they could. Bobbo quite forgot that he wasn't supposed to be there, and ran to meet him too.

The jolly old man swung the children off their feet and hugged them.

'Pleased to see you,' he said. 'What a fine batch of good children this year!'

Then Bobbo remembered. He slipped behind the twins, and said nothing. He was terribly afraid of being found out and sent home before he had seen all he wanted to.

'Come along!' cried Santa Claus. 'There's some hot cocoa and chocolate buns waiting for you. Then we'll all go and visit my toy workshops.'

He led the way into the castle. The children followed him into a great big hall, with a log fire burning at one end. Before the fire was a big fur rug, and the children all sat down on it, and waited for their buns and cocoa. Little brownies ran in with trays full of cups, and soon all the children were drinking and eating, talking and laughing in the greatest excitement.

'Now, have you finished?' asked Santa Claus. 'Well, come along then, all of you. We'll go to the rocking-horse workshop first.'

Off they all trooped. Santa Claus led them down a long passage towards the sound of hammering and clattering. He opened a big door, and there was the rocking-horse workshop!

It was the loveliest place! There were gnomes running about with hammers and paintpots, and everyone was working at top speed.

'Only a week before Christmas,' explained Santa Claus. 'We're very busy just now. I've had so many letters from children asking for rocking-horses this year that I had to have a good many hundreds more made than usual. Go round and see my gnomes at work.'

The children wandered round, watching the busy gnomes. Bobbo went with the golden-haired boy, and they saw the horses being carefully painted. One gnome was very busy sticking fine bushy tails on to the horses, and another one was putting on the manes.

Two little gnomes were doing the nicest work of all. They were going round the workshop, riding first on one horse, then on another, to see if they all rocked properly.

'How do you get the horses on to the sleigh?' asked Bobbo.

'Watch!' said the gnome he spoke to. He climbed up on to a rocking-horse and jerked the reins quickly. At once the horse seemed to come alive, and rocked swiftly forward over the floor before Bobbo could say 'Knife!' It went towards the door all by itself, neighing loudly, while the little gnome waved his hand to Bobbo. All the other horses began to neigh when they heard the first one, and the children stared in astonishment as they saw first one and then another come alive and begin to sway forward. Only those that were not quite finished kept still.

'Catch a rocking-horse and get on to its back!' cried Santa Claus. 'We'll let them take us to my next workshop – where the dolls' houses are made!'

Every child caught hold of a rocking-horse and climbed on to its back. Bobbo got a fine one, painted in red and green with a great bushy tail and mane. He took hold of the reins, and at once the horse rocked quickly forwards, following Santa Claus, who had jumped on to the biggest horse there. Off they all went on their strange horses, and rocked all the way upstairs to another big room.

'Here we are,' said Santa Claus. 'Now see how carefully your dolls' houses are made, children!'

The children jumped off their horses and stared in wonder. The room was full of little fairies, who were doing all sorts of jobs. Some were daintily painting the roof of a dolls' house, and others were cleaning the windows.

There must be thousands and thousands of houses, thought Bobbo, looking round. Oh, there's a fairy putting up curtains! I often wondered who put those tiny curtains up at the windows of dolls' houses!

He went round looking at everything. He saw curtains being put up, knockers being polished, pictures hung, and carpets laid.

'The fairies do all this because they're just the right size to get into the houses nicely,' said Santa Claus. 'Look! Here are some houses being lived in to see if they are quite free from damp, and have been well built.'

The children looked. They had come to one end of the big room, where a whole row of dolls' houses stood side by side. As they looked they saw the front doors open, and out came a number of little fairies.

'We sleep in the beds and see if they are comfortable,' they told the children. 'We cook our dinners on the stove in the kitchen and see if it is all right. We sit on all the chairs to see if they are soft. Then, if they are, we know your dolls will enjoy themselves here. And even if you don't let your dolls live in these houses, well, the fairies who live in your nurseries will often spend a night or two there, and they will be glad to find everything all right.'

Bobbo would have liked to stay there all night, watching the fairies pop in and out of the dolls' houses, but Santa Claus told the children to mount their rocking-horses again, and follow him.

'We'll go to the train workshop now!' he said. And off they all galloped again on their trusty wooden horses, downstairs and round a corner into a great yard.

'My goodness!' said Bobbo, when he got there. 'What a lot of trains!'

There *were* a lot, too! They were all rushing round and round, or up and down, driven by pixies.

'We've finished making all these,' said Santa Claus. 'They're ready to go to children now, but the pixies are just testing them to see that they run all right.'

Bobbo thought it was grand to test toy trains like that. The pixies seemed to be enjoying themselves immensely. They were very clever at driving their little trains, and never bumped into each other. They went under little bridges and past little signals at a terrific rate, their engines dragging behind them a long procession of carriages or trucks.

'Oh, they stop at the little stations!' cried the golden-haired boy. 'Look!'

Sure enough they did! There were tiny stations here and there with metal porters standing by trucks, and metal passengers waiting. And they all came alive when the engine stopped at their station! The porters began wheeling their trucks, and the passengers ran to get in the carriages.

'Oh, isn't it fun!' cried the children. 'How we wish we could ride in a little toy train too!'

'Very well, you can!' laughed Santa Claus. 'The metal ones are too small, but I've a big wooden train and carriages here that will just about take you all. Here it comes.'

The children saw a big red wooden engine coming along, driven by a pixie. It dragged three open wooden carriages behind it, and stopped by Santa Claus.

'Get in!' he said. 'There's room for all of you. We'll go to the next workshop in the train and tell the horses to go back to their own place.'

At once the rocking-horses rocked themselves away, and the children climbed into the carriages of the wooden train. It was just large enough for them, and when they were all in, it trundled away merrily.

It took them to where the clockwork toys were made, and after that to where the red gnomes were making fireworks. Then they went to where the dolls were made, and the teddy bears and soft toys. And soon they had visited so many exciting places that Bobbo began to lose count, and became more excited than ever.

But at last they came to the only place they hadn't seen. This was a big room, in the middle of which a beautiful fairy was sitting. She sat by a well that went deep down into the mountain, so deep that no one knew how deep it was. No one had ever heard a stone reach the bottom.

'Now this,' said Santa Claus, 'is the Wishing Well.'

All the children looked at it in awe.

None of them had seen a wishing well before, and the fairy by it was so beautiful that she almost dazzled their eyes.

'All the good children who come here year by year,' said Santa Claus, 'visit this Well before they go back home. The fairy who owns it gives them one wish. She will give you each one, so think hard before you wish, for whatever your wish is it will come true.'

The children stared at each other, and thought of what they would wish. Then one by one they stepped forwards. The fairy handed them each a little blue stone, and told them to drop it into the Well as they spoke their wish.

The golden-haired boy wished first.

'I wish that my mother may get well before Christmas,' he said.

Then came the twins and they wished together.

'We wish our father could get some work to do,' they wished.

Then came other children, all wishing differently.

'I wish my mummy had lots of nice things for Christmas,' said one.

'I wish my little brother may not be ill any more,' said another.

'I wish all the poor children in my town a big Christmas pudding on Christmas Day,' said a third.

So the wishes went on, until it came to Bobbo's turn. He had been thinking very hard what he would wish for, and being a selfish little boy, he thought of nobody but himself.

He went up to the fairy, and took the blue stone she held out to him. Then he turned to the Well, and dropped it in.

'I wish that on Christmas Day I may have a Christmas stocking that will pour out toys and pets for me without stopping!' he said.

At once there was a dead silence. Everybody stared at Bobbo, and he began to feel uncomfortable.

Then the fairy spoke sadly.

'Alas!' she said. 'I have given a wish to a child who is not good, for he is selfish. He will regret his wish on Christmas Day.'

'No, I shan't,' said Bobbo, feeling very glad to think that his wish wasn't going to be taken from him.

'Come here,' said Santa Claus sternly to Bobbo. The little boy went over to him, and Santa Claus looked at him closely.

'You are not one of this year's good children,' he said. 'How did you get here?'

Bobbo hung his head and told him. Santa Claus frowned heavily, and all the watching children trembled.

'You have done a foolish thing,' said Santa

Claus, 'and your own foolishness will punish you.' Then he turned to the other children.

'It is time to return home,' he told them. 'We are late, so we will not go by the reindeer sleigh this time. The fairy will wish a wish for you.'

'Come near to me,' said the fairy in her silvery voice. 'Take hands, all of you, and sit down on the ground. Shut your eyes and listen to me.'

They all did as they were told, Bobbo too, and shut their eyes to listen. The fairy began to sing them a dreamy, sleepy song, and soon every child's head fell forward, and one by one the children slept.

Bobbo's head dropped forward on to his chest as he heard the fairy's dreamy voice, and soon he was dreaming. He went on dreaming and dreaming and dreaming, and whilst he was dreaming, the fairy, by her magic, took him, and all the other children, back to their faraway beds. But how she did it neither I nor anyone knows.

When Bobbo woke up the next morning he rubbed

his eyes, and suddenly remembered his adventures of the night before.

'I don't think it *could* have been a dream,' he thought. 'What about my slippers? I had those on, and if they are dirty underneath then I shall know I really *did* go out in the snow with them on!'

He jumped out of bed and went to find his slippers. They were standing by the bed, and when he picked them up, he saw that underneath they were not only dirty, but wet too.

'That just proves it!' said Bobbo, in delight. 'Now I shall only have to wait a few days more for my wish to come true. Fancy having a stocking that will pour me out pets and toys without stopping!'

He told nobody about his adventure, and waited impatiently for Christmas Day to come. He wondered where he would find the stocking, and he decided that it would probably be hanging at the end of the bed, where Christmas stockings usually hang.

At last Christmas Eve came. Bobbo went to bed

early so that Christmas Day would come all the sooner. He lay for a long time without going to sleep, for he was feeling very excited.

Then at last his eyes closed and he fell asleep. The night flowed by, and dawn came.

Bobbo woke up about seven o'clock and found a grey light in his bedroom. Day had hardly yet come. He remembered at once what was to happen, and he sat up quickly, his heart thumping in excitement. He gazed at the end of his bed, and saw there the Christmas stocking that his father and mother had given him, full of toys. Down on the floor beside it were lots of parcels, but Bobbo didn't feel a bit interested in them. He wanted to see where the magic stocking was.

Then he saw it. It was a little blue stocking, just the colour of the stone he had thrown down the Wishing Well. It hung on one of the knobs of his bed, and looked as thin and empty as his own stocking did, lying on the chair nearby.

'Oh!' cried Bobbo in disappointment. 'Is that all my magic stocking is going to be?'

He reached over to the foot of the bed, and took the stocking down. Then he had a good look at it. It was tied up at the top with a piece of blue ribbon, and the stocking itself felt as empty as could be.

'There's nothing in it at all!' said Bobbo angrily. 'That fairy told a story!'

He took hold of the ribbon that tied up the top of the stocking, and jerked it undone. It came off the stocking and fell on to the bed. Bobbo turned the stocking upside down, and shook it out on to the pillow, thinking there might perhaps be some little thing inside it.

And then the magic began to work! For out of the stocking suddenly came a kitten that fell on the pillow and began to mew! Then came a box of soldiers, and then a book. Bobbo had no time to look at each thing carefully, for before he had time to pick it up, something else came!

'It's working, it's working!' cried the little boy in the greatest excitement. 'Oh, my goodness, oh, my gracious, it's really, really magic!'

Out came a whole host of things on to his bed! They certainly came from the stocking, though Bobbo could never feel them in there before they appeared. All sorts of things came, big and little, and even a rocking-horse suddenly fell with a thump on to the floor!

Soon Bobbo's bed was covered with toys. The kitten mewed as a ball came tumbling on to its head, and no sooner had it mewed than another kitten came falling down by it, and then a puppy and a little yellow canary.

After the canary came a whole string of white rats, about twenty of them. They ran about all over the place, and squeaked loudly. Bobbo watched them in amazement.

But then something happened that made the little boy begin to feel uncomfortable. The stocking suddenly jerked out of his hand, and began to flap about in a most curious manner, all by itself. Out of it came a long leg, with a hoof at the end. Then another appeared and yet another. The stocking jumped nearly up to the ceiling, and when it came down again, Bobbo saw that a great animal was miraculously falling on to the floor too. And whatever in the world do you think it was?

It was a great white donkey, with long black ears. As soon as it reached the floor, it began to make a most alarming sound.

'Hee-haw, hee-haw!' it went, and stamped on the carpet with its hind feet.

'Oh dear!' cried Bobbo, slipping under the blankets quickly. 'I don't like this. It's too much magic, I think!'

Now Bobbo's father and mother were lying in bed talking, when they suddenly heard the enormous noise made by the donkey in Bobbo's bedroom. Bobbo's father leapt out of bed at once, and his mother sat up in terror.

'Whatever is it?' she cried. 'It sounds as if it's coming from Bobbo's bedroom.'

'I'll go and see,' said his father, and tore down the landing. He flung open the door of Bobbo's room – and then stared in the greatest horror and amazement.

And well he might, for Bobbo's room was full of hundreds and hundreds of things. Toys, big and little, were strewn all over the place, and kittens and puppies were playing madly together. White rats nibbled at the sweets and chocolates down by the bed, and a rabbit was lying on the hearthrug. Worst of all, the donkey stood with its forefeet on the mantelpiece, trying to nibble some carrots in a picture.

Bobbo was nowhere to be seen. He was safely under the blankets, cowering at the bottom of the bed. The stocking lay on the floor, and things jerked themselves out without stopping. Even as Bobbo's horrified father looked, he saw a tortoise come wriggling out, and make its way to where he stood on the mat.

'Oh! Oh!' cried Bobbo's father. 'What is happening

here? Bobbo, Bobbo, where are you? Where have you gone?'

Bobbo answered from the bottom of the bed.

'I'm here,' he said. 'Oh, Daddy, is it you? Come and rescue me from all these things.'

His father stepped over six white rats, stumbled over the rabbit, went round the rocking-horse, trod on a box of fine soldiers, and reached Bobbo. He picked up the little boy, blanket and all, and lifted him up in his arms. Then, nearly falling over a pile of big teddy bears, and squashing two boxes of chocolates, he managed to make his way safely to the door. He carried Bobbo into his mother's room, and told his astonished wife what he had seen.

Even as he spoke, two white rats ran into the room, and Bobbo's mother shrieked in horror. Then the donkey was heard falling downstairs, and two screams from below told the parents that the cook, and the housemaid, had seen him.

'What does it all mean, what does it all mean?'

cried Bobbo's mother. 'Are we dreaming, or is this all real?'

'Bobbo, do you know anything about this?' asked his father. 'How did it all begin?'

Bobbo began to cry, and in between his tears he told the story of how he had been to the home of Santa Claus, pretending to be one of the good children. He told about his wish, and how it had come true that very morning.

'It's all that horrid magic stocking,' wept Bobbo. 'It's lying in my room jerking out things without stopping, just as I wished it to. Oh, why didn't I wish an unselfish wish like all the other children did?'

Bobbo's mother and father listened to the story gravely. They were grieved to think their little boy had not been good enough to be chosen, but had gone all the same, and wished a wish that showed what an unpleasant child he was.

'It's our fault really,' said his father to his mother. 'We have spoilt him, you and I. We have always let him think of himself and never of other people. We must alter all that now.'

'I want to alter it,' said Bobbo. 'I want to be good, but I shan't have a chance now. That horrid stocking will go on and on all my life long!'

'Oh, bless us all, I'd forgotten that stocking would still be going on,' said his father, jumping up. 'Hello, what's that?'

He heard a loud voice shouting up the stairs. It was a policeman!

'Hi, there!' called the deep voice. 'What are you doing, letting your pets out of the house like this? You're frightening all the neighbours! This is a fine sort of Christmas morning to give them. Why, the road's full of puppies, rats, and kittens, to say nothing of rabbits, goats, and a snake or two.'

Bobbo's father waded through pets and toys until he got downstairs. There he saw the indignant policeman, and found that the cook and the housemaid had run out of the house in fright, and had left the front door open, so that all the pets had been able to wander downstairs and outside.

'Are you thinking of starting a zoo?' asked the puzzled policeman, trying to catch a white rat that was running up his trouser leg.

'No,' said Bobbo's father, 'it's magic, I'm afraid.'

'Come on, now!' said the policeman. 'You can't spin a story like that to me!'

A large swan came flying down the stairs and landed on his shoulder. He was so astonished that he fell straight down the front steps with the swan on top of him, and just as he was getting up, something got between his legs, and he sat down on a hedgehog.

That was enough for the policeman. Swans, snakes, hedgehogs, and rats seemed to belong to nightmares, not to Christmas morning, so he got off the hedgehog, and ran for his life to the nearest police station.

'Oh, my!' said Bobbo's father, seeing two large tortoises coming solemnly towards him. 'That stocking must certainly be stopped!'

He ran upstairs, and went to Bobbo.

'How can you stop that stocking from sending out any more things?' he asked.

'I don't know,' said Bobbo, miserably. 'But perhaps Nancy, the little girl next door, might know. She was one of the good children who were taken to Santa Claus.'

Bobbo's father tore downstairs again, knocking over a duck on the way, and ran to Nancy's house. She was at the front door, watching the things coming out of Bobbo's house, and Bobbo's father told her everything.

'Yes, I think I know how to stop the stocking,' she said. 'Santa Claus told me, in case Bobbo was sorry about his wish. But is he *really* sorry?'

'He certainly is,' said Bobbo's father. 'This has taught us all something, and you may be sure Bobbo won't have a chance to be a horrid, selfish little boy again. He doesn't want to be, either.'

Nancy went to Bobbo's house straightaway. She

picked her way through the animals and came to Bobbo's room, which was full right to the ceiling with toys and pets. The stocking was still performing on a mat near the door, and the little girl pounced on it.

'Where's the ribbon that tied it up?' she asked. 'Oh, there it is!'

She picked up the blue ribbon. Then she held the stocking toe downwards, and shook it violently three times.

At once a strange thing happened. All the toys and animals came rushing towards it, and one by one they took a jump at the stocking, and seemed to disappear inside it. Even the donkey vanished in that way, though Bobbo's father couldn't for the life of him think how. The stocking jerked and jumped as the things disappeared, and very soon the room became quite empty-looking. Still Nancy held the stocking, and then gradually the whole room, stairs and hall were emptied of their toys and animals. All the pets that had wandered into the street came back too, and at last nothing was left at all except the stocking, which lay quiet and still in Nancy's hand.

She took the piece of blue ribbon, and tied it firmly round the mouth of the stocking. Then she gave the stocking to Bobbo's father.

'There you are,' she said. 'It's quite safe now.'

'Thank you, Nancy,' said Bobbo's father, gratefully. 'I'll keep it in Bobbo's nursery, just to remind of him of what happens to selfish children.'

He carried it in to Bobbo, and told the little boy what Nancy had done.

'Now you'd better make up your mind to turn over a new leaf, and try to be good enough to be chosen properly to go on the trip to Santa Claus's home,' he said.

'I will,' said Bobbo, and he meant it. 'I'll begin this very day, and I'll take my nicest toys to the poor children in the hospital.'

Bobbo kept his word, and tried his best to be different. He didn't find it easy, but because he had plenty of pluck, he managed it – and you'll be glad to know that the very next Christmas he was awakened one night, and what should he see outside but the reindeer sleigh full of happy laughing children!

'Come on, come on!' cried the elf. 'You really are one of us this time, Bobbo!'

And off they all went with a jingling of bells over the deep white snow!

The Pantomime Wolf

The Pantomime Wolf

THE SCHOOL was breaking up for the Christmas holidays and all the children were excited.

'I'm having a fine Christmas party!' said Ann. 'I'm having a Christmas tree that will touch the ceiling!'

'I'm having a new bicycle for Christmas,' said Peter.

'We're going to the pantomime,' said Jane and Leslie, the twins.

'Are *you* doing anything exciting?' Peter asked Tom and Shirley. They had been putting on their boots and hadn't said anything.

'Nothing much,' said Tom. 'Mother's been ill and she hasn't been able to arrange anything for us yet.'

'Bad luck!' said Peter. 'Well – happy holidays to you! Goodbye!'

All the children ran off home. Tom and Shirley went, too. They passed a big poster showing Red Riding-hood and the Wolf.

'The pantomime this year is Red Riding-hood and the Wolf,' said Shirley. 'I do wish we could see it. But I'm sure Mother won't be able to afford it, Tom – so we'd better not ask her.'

'She hasn't paid the doctor's bill yet,' said Tom. 'We can't expect much this Christmas, Shirley, with Daddy away, and Mother only just getting better.'

So they were very good indeed, and didn't ask for a party or a Christmas tree, or to go to the circus or the pantomime. Mother thought they were very unselfish and she did wish she could give them all the treats they wanted. But she couldn't.

The other children went to the pantomime, and when they met Shirley and Tom they told them about it.

'It's *wonderful*!' said Peter. You should just see the old wolf!'

'And Red Riding-hood is lovely,' said Ann. 'The old grandmother was funny. She made me laugh. And the woodland scene is gorgeous, Shirley – you'd love it, because fairies fly among the trees. It looks exactly as if they *are* flying, but my daddy says they are on wires.'

The more Shirley and Tom heard about the pantomime the more they longed to see it. They opened their money-box to see if by any chance they had enough for tickets; but no, they had spent nearly all their money at Christmas-time for presents, and there were only a few pennies left.

'I wonder if we could earn some money by doing errands,' said Tom suddenly. 'If people gave us a penny here and there, we might *just* get enough before the pantomime is over.'

So they began to run errands for people the very next day. They took the washing out for old Mrs

Brown and she gave them a penny a time. They fetched the shopping for Miss Lucy and she gave them two pence each. They took Mr Jones' dog for a walk three evenings running and he gave them a penny each time, too.

Very soon they had nearly enough money. They felt very pleased with themselves. Tom put all the money into a little leather purse and kept it in his pocket.

The day before the pantomime was performed for the very last time the children had just enough money. They counted it out in the street after they had been running errands all day and were really very tired.

'Just enough for the cheapest seats of all,' said Tom, pleased. 'Isn't that good, Shirley? We've just got it in time, because the pantomime stops after tomorrow. We'll go on the last night. That will be fun!'

Now on their way home a dreadful thing happened. Tom put his hand into his pocket to make sure the purse of money was there – and it wasn't! It was gone!

His pocket was empty and there was an enormous hole at the bottom.

'Shirley! Oh, Shirley! The purse is gone!' cried Tom, and he went quite pale. It had taken them so long to earn the money – and now it was gone.

'Tom! How dreadful! We must go back up the road at once to find it,' said Shirley. They turned back – and oh, how they hunted and hunted for that lost purse. But they couldn't find it anywhere. It was quite gone. Someone must have picked it up.

Very sadly indeed the two children turned to go home again. Shirley was crying. They had both worked so hard. Now there was no money – and no pantomime.

'I had looked forward to it so much,' said Shirley: Tom slipped his arm through hers.

'Shirley, it's my fault the money was lost,' he said. 'I knew there was a hole coming in my pocket. I'm terribly, terribly sorrry. Don't cry.'

But Shirley did cry. She was very tired, and now there was no pantomime to think about and look forward to. The two children went home in the twilight, feeling cold and miserable.

A man passed them on a motorbike. He made a great noise, and the children looked after him as he passed. They saw that he had a big bundle on the carrier behind – and as they looked, the bundle leapt off the bike and fell into the road.

The man on the motorbike didn't stop. He hadn't noticed that the bundle had fallen off. *Chug-chug-chug*, his bike went down the road at a great speed.

'Look – he's dropped something!' said Tom. 'Hi, hi, you've dropped something!'

But the man was round the corner, and didn't hear Tom's shout. The children went to pick up the bundle. It had burst and was lying in a big patch on the road. Shirley gave a scream.

'Tom! It's an animal! Oh, Tom, what is it? Look at its big head!'

'What big ears its got!' said Tom, looking at the large animal-head.

'And what big eyes its got!' said Shirley, trembling. 'And oh, what *big* teeth its got, Tom!'

'We sound like the story of Red Riding-hood, don't we?' said Tom, laughing. 'Cheer up, Shirley. Don't look so frightened. It isn't alive.'

'It looks alive in this half-darkness,' said Shirley, not going very near. 'It's got a big furry body, and a long tail, Tom. What is it?'

'A wolf,' said Tom. 'And do you know what I think, Shirley? I think it's the wolf-skin that the man wears who is the big wolf in Red Riding-hood! I believe that was the man on his way to the evening performance of the pantomime!'

'Oh, I say – whatever will he do when he finds he has lost his wolf-skin?' cried Shirley. 'That's worse than losing a purse of money! He won't be able to wear his skin and be the wolf – there won't be any pantomime tonight if there isn't a wolf!'

'We'd better go to the Town Hall, where the pantomime is performed each night, and take it back to the wolf-man,' said Tom.

'Oh, dear,' said Shirley. 'That's such a long way, Tom, and I'm so tired and miserable.'

'Well, I'll take it by myself, darling,' said Tom, feeling sorry for his tired little sister.

'No; it's too heavy for you to carry all that way by yourself,' said Shirley. 'I'll come, too. Of course, I will.'

So the two of them carried the heavy wolf-skin through the streets together. Tom carried the head end and Shirley carried the tail end. She said she didn't like the head much, with its staring eyes and big teeth.

They came at last to the Town Hall and went up the steps. The hall porter there stared at them in surprise. 'What do *you* want?' he said.

'We want the wolf-man,' said Tom. 'We found his wolf-skin in the road.'

'My word, he *will* be pleased!' said the man. He said it had fallen off his carrier, and he's sent someone to see if they can find it. He's in a dreadful state, and so is everyone, because the pantomime can't begin without the wolf!'

The man took the children down a long passage, down some steps, and then along another passage, very dark and cold. He came to a door and knocked.

'Come in!' said a deep voice, and the children went in, carrying the big wolf-skin between them. There was a small man inside the little room, and when he saw the children and the skin he leapt to his feet with a shout.

'My wolf-skin! Thank goodness! Where did you find it? Bless you a thousand times for bringing it. I took it home for my sister to mend for me, and it must have dropped off the back of my bike.'

'Yes, it did. We saw it,' said Tom. 'I'm very glad we were able to bring it to you in time for the performance tonight.'

The man quickly got into the skin and asked Shirley to zip him up. She zipped him, thinking how funny it was to run a zip up a wolf's tummy like that.

The man didn't put the head on. He said it was too hot, and he let it hang down the back of the skin.

'How do you like the pantomime?' he asked. 'Do you like it when I do my funny dance?'

'We haven't seen the pantomime,' said Tom, and he told the wolf-man all about how his mother had been ill, and how he and Shirley had earned money, and how he had lost it that evening. 'And so, you see, we can't see your pantomime now,' said Tom, sadly.

'That's just where you make a mistake!' said the wolf-man, heartily. 'Of course you are going to see it! You go straight home to your mother, and tell her that you two are to come here with her tomorrow night, and sit in the Very Front Row! You deserve a reward. Now you go home and tell her that!'

Well! That was simply marvellous!

'We wouldn't have been able to have any but the cheapest seats – and now we shall have the Very Front Row!' said Tom, happily, as they went home to tell their mother.

She could hardly believe her ears. She kissed them both. 'You really do deserve a treat,' she said. 'You've been such good, unselfish children, and haven't grumbled at all – and you did work so hard to earn some money. I was very proud of you.'

They went to the pantomime the next night and, as the wolf-man had promised, they had seats in the Very Front Row. They did feel grand.

It was a lovely pantomime – but the nicest part of all was when the wolf waved his paw to Tom and Shirley. They felt prouder than they had ever felt in their lives before!

'Good old wolf!' cried Tom. 'You're as bad as can be in the pantomime – but I'm going to give you the biggest clap of all, all the same!'

Little Mrs Millikin

Little Mrs Millikin

MRS MILLIKIN was a tiny old lady who lived in Nod village. She hadn't any children of her own, so she loved everybody else's. She loved little Peter who lived at the grocer's. She loved Susie Green who lived at the post-office. She loved the baby next door, and she loved the twins across the road, although they were really very naughty sometimes.

And they all loved little Mrs Millikin. When they saw her coming they ran to her, shouting, 'Millikin! Millikin! Have you got a sweet for us? Millikin, tell us a story!'

Mrs Millikin spent all her money on sweets and

toys for other people's children. She made chocolate biscuits every week to put into a tin that she kept for the children when they came to see her. She remembered all their birthdays and bought them cards and presents.

So they loved her very much, and when the twins made her a pin-cushion for her birthday little Mrs Millikin was so proud of it that she showed it to quite a hundred people. She kept it in the middle of her mantelpiece and hardly dared to put a pin or needle in it for fear of spoiling it.

Of course, you can imagine then when Christmas-time came Mrs Millikin went quite mad. She spent all her money on things like balloons and crackers and toys and sweets, and gave them to all the children she knew. She saved up for weeks before so that she could have a really good spend.

Then what a time she had! She went to the toyshop and bought dolls, toys, and books. She went to the sweet-shop and bought packets of sweets and boxes of chocolate and tins of biscuits. She went to the book-shop and bought all kinds of cheerful cards. Really, she had a perfectly lovely time – but she was happiest of all when she gave what she had bought to the children, and heard all their squeals of joy and saw their beaming faces.

'That's my best Christmas present,' she always said. 'That's my very best Christmas present – seeing the children so happy and excited.'

Now one Christmas little Mrs Millikin planned all her presents as usual. Ships for the twins. A doll for Susie Green – one that opened and shut its eyes. Books for Bobby. A rattle for the baby. Oh, she would have a fine time spending all her money!

Little Mrs Millikin worked very hard to get her money. She scrubbed Mrs Jones's floors for her. She washed Mrs Lacy's curtains. She mended Mr Timm's socks. And by the time Christmas week came she had a purse full of money to spend. So out she went to spend it at the toyshop and the sweet-shop.

And then a really dreadful thing happened! Little Mrs Millikin had a hole in her skirt pocket and she didn't know it! She put her purse there, and as she walked along to the village, the purse dropped out. Mrs Millikin didn't hear it fall, so she didn't know.

When she got to the toyshop she put her hand into her pocket to get out her purse – and it wasn't there! What a shock for her! The tiny old lady ran back along the road to see if she could find it. But she couldn't find it anywhere.

And no wonder she couldn't – for Jim the tramp had spied it on the ground and had picked it up in joy. He had gone off with it, thinking that he would buy himself a really fine Christmas dinner. So little Mrs Millikin didn't find her purse at all. She was very unhappy.

'Now I can't buy the children any presents,' she thought, with tears in her eyes. 'The twins must do without their ships – and oh, I did promise to give them one each! And Susie can't have her doll. This is really dreadful!'

She did not think that she would not have any Christmas dinner herself. She had meant to buy something for her own dinner on Christmas Day – now she would have to have bread and jam. But all she worried about was not being able to buy presents for the children.

She went to bed very unhappy on Christmas Eve. She had a very little bed, because she was a very little person. It was a cold night, so she drew the blanket right over her head to keep warm. She didn't go to sleep for a long time, but at last she shut her eyes and fell fast asleep.

Now, as you know, Santa Claus comes along each Christmas Eve and fills the children's stockings with toys. He doesn't bother about the grown-ups, of course – they can buy all they want for themselves.

Well, this Christmas Eve, quite by mistake, Santa Claus went down the wrong chimney. He thought he was going down Susie Green's chimney and he wasn't. He was going down little Mrs Millikin's!

When he got down into her bedroom he stared round. This wasn't Susie Green's room. He must have come down the wrong chimney. What a nuisance!

Then he caught sight of little Mrs Millikin lying on her little tiny bed. She was a very small person, no bigger than a child, and as she had the blanket pulled right up to her hair, Santa Claus couldn't see that she wasn't a child. He quite thought she was, she was so small!

'Now here's a funny thing!' said Santa to himself, turning over the pages of his notebook, till he came to the names of all the children in Nod village. 'Here's a very – funny – thing! I haven't got this child's name down! How lucky that I happened to come down the chimney! This child would have had no presents from me if I hadn't come along tonight by mistake. And that would have been a great pity.'

Santa Claus stared at the bed. He wondered if it

was a boy or a girl. He didn't know. He couldn't see the face of the sleeping person. He didn't like to pull down the blanket in case he woke up the sleeper.

'Well, I don't really know what to do,' said Santa, scratching his head and frowning. 'It may be a boy. It may be a girl. It may even be a baby, though it looks rather too big for that. What had I better do? And where's the stocking for me to fill? There doesn't seem to *be* one. So I simply can't tell what child it is – boy, girl, or baby!'

He looked round the little bedroom. He saw a pair of old Mr Timm's socks that Mrs Millikin had just washed and darned, and had put ready to take back to him.

'Good!' he said. 'Those will do nicely.' He unrolled them and hung them at the foot of the little bed. Then he undid his sack and looked inside.

'If it's a boy it will like ships and boats,' he said, and he put a ship and a boat into a stocking. 'If it's a girl it will like dolls.' He put a beautiful doll into the stocking, so that it peeped out at the top. It could open and shut its eyes and it had golden curls and a blue ribbon.

'If it's a baby it will like a rattle,' said Santa, and into the stocking went a blue-and-red rattle. Then old Santa dived into his sack again and brought out some books, and an engine, and a race-game.

'I didn't give this child anything at all last year,' he thought. 'Poor little thing! I'd better make up for it this year.'

So he packed into those two big stockings all sorts of lovely things – sweets, biscuits, oranges, nuts, apples, little animals, balls, and even a toy telephone, which he knew most children really loved.

Then up the chimney he went again, and disappeared into the frosty night. Mrs Millikin heard the bells of the reindeer in her dreams but they didn't wake her up. She didn't open her eyes till the morning – and then how she stared *and* stared!

At the bottom of her bed hung two large stockings.

From one peeped a pretty, golden-haired doll. From the other stared a large wooden soldier.

'I must still be asleep,' said Mrs Millikin. 'Or else I've gone back to being a child. Which is it?'

She got out of bed and looked at herself in the glass. No – she was still Mrs Millikin, with curly grey hair and a wrinkled, smiling face!

But it wasn't a dream either. '*Most* peculiar,' thought Mrs Millikin, looking at the stockings again. 'It almost looks as if Santa Claus has been here and filled those stockings for me. What shall I do about it?'

And then, of course, she knew quite well what she was going to do about it!

'I'll give all the toys to the children!' she cried. 'How pleased they will be! Here are just the things they want – a ship – a boat – an engine – a doll – a rattle – oh, what marvellous things, to be sure!'

You would have been surprised to see how quickly Mrs Millikin dressed that morning. She was out of the house in fifteen minutes, carrying all the toys. And what a wonderful time she had giving away all those presents! How the children hugged and kissed her!

'What have you got for your Christmas dinner, Mrs Millikin?' asked Susie Green, hugging her doll in joy. 'We've got turkey and plum pudding. Ooooooh!'

'Well, I've got bread and jam, and that's all,' said Mrs Millikin. 'But I shall be just as happy with that as you will with your turkey and plum pudding – because, you see, I've seen so many smiling faces this morning that they are as good as a feast to me.'

'Millikin, you must stay and share my dinner!' said Susie. 'Mustn't she, Mummy? Do say yes.'

'Of course she must!' said Mummy. And Mrs Millikin had to. Then she went to tea with Bobby, and shared his Christmas tree, so she had a marvellous Christmas after all.

'Best I've ever had!' she said to herself, as she

cuddled down into her small bed that night. 'Best I've ever had. And I'm sure I don't know what I've done to deserve it.'

But I know quite a lot of things, don't you?

Second Walk
in December

Second Walk
in December

BEFORE CHRISTMAS the children went out together, and cut down holly boughs, scarlet with berries, and a big tuft of mistletoe from the oak tree. They carried them home, looking like children on a Christmas card, with the holly over their shoulders.

They decorated Uncle Merry's study and it looked so bright and Christmassy. Each of the children had brought a present for him. They wrapped up the presents in paper, wrote loving messages, and left them on Uncle Merry's table. He was not coming back till Christmas Eve.

'I hope he'll like the new walking stick I bought,' said Pat. 'I chose it very carefully. It's got a nice crooky handle for dragging down catkin branches and things like that.'

'I've embroidered M for Merry on a big white hanky as nicely as ever I could,' said Janet.

'You needn't tell us that again,' said Pat. 'We've seen you doing it for at least three weeks!'

'I don't think much of my present for him, really,' said John, thinking that the others had bought Uncle Merry very nice presents indeed. 'I've only got this new notebook for him and a *very* sharp pencil. It's to put down his notes about birds. I saw that his notebook was old and almost full.'

'He'll like the painting of a bird you've made on the cover,' said Janet. 'You did it beautifully. It's just like the kingfisher we saw by the stream.'

It was dark when the children got back to their own house. Their mother met them, looking quite sad.

'Children, the Christmas tree hasn't come! You know, the one they sent was too small, so I sent it back – and the greengrocer promised to send another. Now I hear that he hasn't any left at all.'

This was sad news indeed. No Christmas tree! Oh dear, what a pity! Mother was sad, too, because she had so much looked forward to dressing the tree in its bright ornaments and candles that evening, when the children had gone to bed.

'Never mind,' said Janet. 'We'll get one after Christmas, and dress it then.'

Christmas morning dawned brilliantly. The boys couldn't think why their bedroom was so full of dazzling white light. But Janet soon told them!

'It's snowed in the night! Oh, come and look, Pat and John! Everywhere is buried in thick white snow!'

The countryside was beautiful in its white mantle. The garden was very still. Everything was softened by the dazzling snow. The children were thrilled.

'Just exactly right for Christmas Day!' they said,

and rushed to see what was in their stockings. They made such a noise that their mother came to enjoy the fun.

'What excitement!' she said. 'Do you like your presents?'

'Oh *yes*!' cried the children, and ran to give her a Christmas hug.

'Uncle Merry came in last night after you had gone to bed,' said Mother. 'He is back again. He was sad to hear that we hadn't a Christmas tree. He is coming in after breakfast with a present for you all.'

'Oh, how lovely!' said Janet. 'Oh, Mother, where did I put my present for Fergus? It's a most wonderful collar, with a plaid pattern all round it – just right for a Scottie dog!'

She soon found it. John found his present for Fergus too – an enormous bone. Pat had a drinking bowl for him with DOG on it. 'Now the cat will know it isn't hers,' said John, when he saw it. That made the others laugh.

'I suppose you think the cat can read?' said Janet.

Uncle Merry came staggering into the garden after breakfast, carrying such a heavy load! Over one shoulder was a perfectly lovely Christmas tree, and over the other a funny thing with one stout leg.

'Happy Christmas, happy Christmas!' shouted everyone, and Fergus wuffed exactly as if he were saying 'Happy Christmas' too!

'I went out and dug up a nice little Christmas tree for you out of my garden this morning,' said Uncle Merry, panting. 'It *was* hard work – but I couldn't bear to think of three nice children like you without any Christmas tree on Christmas Day!'

'Oh, *thank* you, Uncle Merry!' cried the children. 'It's a beauty! We'll plant it back in your garden again when we've finished with it.'

The spruce fir was put into a big tub, and stood in the hall, ready to be decorated. Then Uncle Merry took the children out into the garden to see the present he had made for them.

'It's between you all,' he said, 'and I hope it will give you much pleasure for years to come. It's the bird-table I promised you!'

'Oh, how lovely!' said Janet, looking at the strong table with its one tall leg. 'Uncle, it's so nice and big. Oh, I'm longing to see some birds on it!'

They dug a hole for the leg, and Uncle Merry rammed it in. Then the table was firm, and was just too high for the cat to jump up on it. Fergus whined and tried to stand up against the pole, but he was far too short to see on the table. He was wearing his new collar, and was very proud of it. He had had a drink out of his new bowl, and a nibble at his bone, so he was very happy. He had had a good look at the letters D-O-G on his bowl, and John felt certain he knew what the word said!

Uncle Merry was delighted with his lovely presents. He wore Janet's hanky in his breast pocket, and he put John's notebook into his inside pocket straight away. 'Just what I want,' he said, 'and as for

Pat's stick, I shall have to take it out this afternoon.'

They nailed twigs at the back of the bird-table, and bound sprays of hips and haws tightly to them. They spread the table with other berries, and seeds that Uncle Merry had either bought or collected.

'We'll buy some peanuts for the tits, and string them on a thread, through their shells,' said Uncle Merry. 'And I wonder if we could spare one or two potatoes cooked in their jackets. The birds love those.'

Soon the table was spread with food of all kinds. No birds flew down to it, though, much to the children's disappointment. They sat at the window, munching bars of chocolate, which Fergus had given to them for Christmas.

Janet suddenly gave a little squeal. 'Uncle Merry! There's a sparrow! I'm sure he's going to fly down to the table!'

The inquisitive little brown bird was sitting on a nearby twig, looking at the spread table with his head cocked knowingly on one side. What was this?

He would fly down and see.

He flew down on to the table, and began to peck at the boiled potato. Then another sparrow flew down and yet another.

The robin flew down to the twigs nailed behind the table, and watched for a chance to hop down, take a beakful of food and hop back again. He didn't like feeding with the noisy sparrows.

Then a big freckled thrush came, and the blackbird. They pecked greedily at the potato, and ran at the sparrows to frighten them away.

A chaffinch came, and then a bluetit. The watching children were really thrilled. 'Oh, Uncle Merry,' said John, 'this is a grand present you've given us! We shall simply love watching the table day after day.'

'You must put a bowl of water on the table too,' said Uncle Merry. 'The birds suffer a good deal from thirst in the winter-time. The water will freeze up, of course, but you can renew it each morning, and the birds will soon learn to come and take a sip when you have put it out.'

Christmas dinner was fun. The turkey was enormous, and the Christmas pudding was set alight so that it flamed brightly when it was carried in. Everyone was glad to have Uncle Merry there, and as for Fergus, he had the time of his life. He sat close by John's legs under the table, and eagerly ate all the titbits that John passed down to him.

'Really, John!' said his mother, in surprise, when he asked for another helping of turkey, 'I have never known you eat such a big dinner!'

After dinner they put on hats and coats and went for a walk. First they hunted under the snow for the Christmas roses, and found five of them out, hiding under the white blanket. It was sweet to see them there. John ran indoors to give them to his mother.

'We really and truly shan't see any flowers in the countryside today,' said Pat, as they trudged down the snowy lane. 'I doubt if we shall see anything, shall we, Uncle Merry, except a few birds? Surely no animal will be out today!'

But although they saw no animal at all, not even a rabbit, they saw where many creatures had been. The snow showed their footprints very clearly indeed. It was John who noticed them first.

'Look!' he said, 'are these a rabbit's prints, Uncle? There are some round marks for his front-paws, and some longer ones where his strong hind-legs touched the snow.'

'Yes,' said Uncle Merry, 'you will find plenty of rabbit footprints about here. The bunnies will come to gnaw the bark of these ivy-stems if the snow stays for long, because the grass they usually nibble will be hidden.'

By the pond the children found marks of webbed feet in the snow. 'Ducks,' said Janet, at once. 'And look, Uncle, you can easily see which footprints are made by hopping birds or walking birds, can't you?'

'How can you tell?' asked Pat, looking at them.

'Because hopping birds put their feet side by side,

and walking birds put them one after the other as we do,' said Janet. 'I should have thought you would have guessed that, silly!'

They examined all the footprints they came to, and it was really very exciting. They saw where the pheasants had roosted, and left the marks of their tails. They discovered where a stoat had chased a frightened rabbit, his neat, round little marks mingled with the prints of the scampering bunny.

'What's this? Is it a dog or a cat?' asked Janet, pointing to a line of footprints on the snowy hillside. Uncle Merry shook his head.

'Not a cat, because she draws in her claws when she walks, and you can see the claw-marks in these clear snow-prints,' he said. 'Not a dog, because you can see here and there where a tail has brushed the snow – a big tail too!'

The children stared at the prints. John suddenly guessed the owner of the marks. 'A fox, of course,' he said. 'Isn't it, Uncle? A fox! He stood here on the hillside watching the rabbits at play, his tail brushing the snow behind him. Uncle Merry, there's quite a story in some of these footprints!'

'There is,' agreed Uncle Merry. 'Hallo, Fergus! Did you think it was time to go home? Poor old fellow, your short legs soon get tired, floundering over the snow, don't they?'

'He makes wonderful snow-prints,' said John. 'Look – quite deep ones – and he shows his claws in them nicely. All right, Fergus, we'll go home to tea.'

Fergus was glad. He was not built for walking in the snow. He found it very difficult to wade along, for he sank almost to his body in the snow. He turned to go home, wagging his tail hard. He wanted to get back to that beautiful bone that John had given him!

'I can see now how the evergreen trees hold the snow,' said Janet, as they went home. 'Look at that silver fir, Uncle – one of its boughs is almost breaking.'

'The other trees, which have lost their leaves, have hardly any snow on at all,' said Pat. 'It has slipped off.'

They soon reached home, shook the snow off their boots, and went indoors. The first thing they saw was the Christmas tree that Uncle Merry had brought for them. It was in the hall, and Mother had decorated it whilst they had been out. It was simply beautiful!

'Oh, Mother! Can we light the candles?' cried Janet. 'Oh, how the ornaments shine, and all the frost you have sprinkled over the branches!'

Uncle Merry lit the candles, and at once the little fir tree became a magic tree, gleaming softly from head to foot in the hall. It was lovely to see. The fairy doll at the top looked down at the children. Fergus looked up at the tree wonderingly. He had seen many trees in his doggy life, but never one that grew lighted candles and shining ornaments!

Christmas Day came to an end at last. The children hugged Uncle Merry when he said goodnight.

'We've had such a happy year,' said Janet, 'all because of you, Uncle Merry. We've learnt to know and love a thousand different things; and now we've begun, we shall go on.'

'Yes,' said John shyly, 'the biggest present you've given us is the key of the countryside, Uncle!'

'A very sweet thing to say!' said Uncle Merry, giving the little boy a hug. 'Well, there's one thing about *that* key, John – once you've got it, you never, never lose it! Goodnight!'

'Wuff!' said Fergus, following his master out into the darkness of the front garden.

'He says "Good night and happy dreams,"' said Janet. 'Same to you, Fergus. Good night. Uncle Merry, goodnight!'

The Magic Snow-Bird

The Magic
Snow-Bird

IT WAS HOLIDAY time, when mothers were giving lots of parties. Jim and Mollie had been asked to a great many, and they were very much looking forward to them. They had been to one, and then a dreadful thing happened! Baby caught chicken-pox – and that meant no more parties for Mollie and Jim in case they caught it too.

Wasn't it unlucky! They were *so* disappointed. Mollie cried, and Jim nearly did, but not quite. There was to be a Christmas tree at the next two parties they had been asked to, and now they would miss all the fun. It was too bad.

'Well, it's no use making a fuss,' said Mother. 'You can't go and you must be brave about it. We are all very sorry for you. Look, I believe it's going to snow! You will be able to play at snowballing soon.'

Sure enough, the snow was falling thickly. Mollie and Jim went to the window and watched it. It came down like big goose feathers, soft and silent. Soon the garden was covered in a white sheet.

The next morning there was about fifteen centimetres of snow everywhere, and the two children shouted with delight.

'We'll build a snowman! We'll snowball the paper-boy! We'll build a little snow-hut!'

'Put on your wellington boots, your thick coats, and woolly caps,' said Mother. 'Then you can go and do what you like.'

So out they went. How lovely it was! Their feet made big marks in the snow, and when they kicked it, it flew up into the air like powder.

'Let's build a snowman first,' said Jim. So they began. They made big balls of snow by rolling them down the lawn. They got bigger and bigger, and then, when they were nice and large, Jim used them for the snowman's body.

They put a hat on his head, and a pipe in his mouth, stones down his front for buttons, and old gloves on his snowy hands. He did look funny. Mother laughed when she saw him.

'Now what shall we make,' asked Jim. 'What about a snow-bird, Mollie? Do you remember how we made a bird at school out of clay? It was quite easy. Let's make a big one out of snow!'

'Yes, nobody makes snow-birds!' said Mollie. 'How surprised everyone will be!'

So they began. First they made a round body. Then they put the bird's long neck on. After that they made a head with a beak of wood sticking out. Then they gave him a long tail sweeping down to the ground.

He stood on two wooden legs, and had two stones for eyes, so he looked very grand indeed.

'Isn't he wonderful!' cried Mollie. 'Just look at him, Jim! Let's call Daddy and Mummy, they'll be so surprised.'

They went to call them, and soon Father and Mother came out into the garden to see the bird. They thought he was magnificent.

Now, just at that very moment a bright blue kingfisher flashed by. He had come from the river, and was going to a nice pool he knew, which he hoped would not be quite frozen over. As he passed over the snow-bird, he dropped one of his blue feathers. It floated down, and stuck in the snow-bird's head, just on the top, so that he looked as if he had a funny little crest.

'Oh, look!' cried Mollie. 'He's got a blue feather on his top-knot! Doesn't he look funny!'

'Leave it,' said Mother. 'Kingfishers' feathers are lucky.'

So they left it, and went in to dinner. It was still there when they went out to play afterwards. This time they made a nice little hut with a door and window. It was just big enough for the two of them. Jim and Mollie were sorry when the sun went and the garden began to get dark.

'We shall have to go in to tea soon,' said Jim, looking out of the little snow-window. Then he suddenly said 'Oh!' and sat very still, staring hard.

'What's the matter?' said Mollie.

'Ssh!' said Jim, in a whisper. 'Keep still. I saw something strange.'

'Oh, *what*?' asked Mollie. 'Quick, tell me.'

'I thought I saw the snow-bird stretch its wings,' said Jim, in astonishment. 'But look – he's quite still now, isn't he, Mollie?'

'Yes, quite,' said Mollie. 'Oh, Jim! Did you really see that?'

'Well, I *thought* I did,' said Jim. 'Let's watch and see if he moves again.'

They watched quietly for a few minutes and then they were called in to tea, and in they had to go. They told Mother what they thought had happened, and she laughed.

'Well, maybe that kingfisher's feather has put some magic into the snow-bird,' she said. 'Everybody knows that there's something magical about kingfishers' feathers.'

'That must be it!' thought the two children. 'What a funny thing!'

After tea they went to the nursery window, and tried to see out into the garden. It was dark, but they could just make out the snowman, the snow-hut and the snow-bird. As they peered out into the darkness, they heard a peculiar noise.

'It sounds like some sort of bird,' said Mollie. '*Could* it be the snow-bird whistling, Jim? It's a kind of singing-whistling noise all mixed up.'

'Let's go and see,' said Jim. So they scrambled down from the window, and ran to put on their coats.

Then they slipped out into the garden.

'Yes, it *is* the snow-bird!' said Jim, in astonishment. 'It must be magic, Mollie.'

They went close up to him. He gleamed white in the darkness, and his two stoney eyes shone brightly.

'Look!' said Jim, 'he's opening and shutting his wings! He's come alive!'

The snow-bird stared at them solemnly. He stood first on one leg, and then on the other. Then he flapped his white wings, and stood on tiptoe.

'Hello, hello, hello!' he said. 'It's nice of you to come and see me. I was just feeling rather lonely.'

'Are you magic?' asked Mollie, who was just a bit frightened.

'I am rather,' answered the bird. 'It's all because of that kingfisher's feather, you know. It's very lucky, and it's very magic. It would make anything come alive!'

'Are you going to fly away?' asked Jim. 'Where will you go to, if you do?'

'All snow-birds, snowmen, and snow-animals belong to the country of the North Wind,' said the bird. 'It's a fine land too. It's where Santa Claus lives, you know. The toys are made there by goblins and dwarfs, the Christmas trees grow there, already decorated with toys—'

'What! Do they grow with toys on them?' cried the children. '*We've* only seen the kind that you buy, and dress up with toys yourself.'

'Pooh,' said the bird. 'Those are stupid. You should just see the ones that grow out in the country of the North Wind! I shall see some tonight, if I go.'

'We were going to some parties where there would be lovely Christmas trees covered with toys,' said Jim. 'But now Baby's got chicken-pox, and we can't. I do wish we could go with you, and see some trees growing with toys already on them.'

'Well, why not?' said the bird, spreading its white wings. 'There's plenty of room on my back, isn't there? You can both sit there comfortably, whilst I fly. I'll bring you back safely enough.'

'Oh!' cried both children in delight. 'What an adventure!'

'You may find me rather cold to sit on,' said the bird. 'I'm made of snow, you know. You'd better get a cushion to put on my back, then you won't feel cold.'

Jim ran to the house and fetched a big cushion from his bedroom. He popped it on the snow-bird's back, and then he and Mollie climbed on. The bird spread its wings, and then *whoosh!* he rose into the air!

Mollie and Jim held on tight. Their hearts were beating very fast, but they were enjoying themselves enormously.

The bird went at a fearful rate, and the children had to pull their woolly caps well down over their ears. They looked downwards, but the earth was too dark for them to see anything except little spots of light here and there.

After a long time, the bird turned its head round to them.

'Nearly there!' he said. 'Isn't this fun!'

'Yes!' shouted the children. 'Oh look! Everything is getting lighter. The sun is rising!'

'Yes, we've gone so fast and far that we've met him again!' said the bird. 'I'm going to land now, so hold tight. You'll be able to see everything quite well soon.'

Down he went, and down. Then *bump*! he landed on the snowy ground. Jim and Mollie jumped off his back. There was sunlight everywhere and they could see everything clearly.

'We haven't much time,' said the snow-bird. 'This is where the goblins live who make the rocking-horses for you.'

He took the children to some big caves in a nearby hill, and Jim and Mollie saw hundreds of tiny goblins busily hammering, painting and putting rockers and manes on fine rocking-horses. The funny thing was that the horses seemed alive, and neighed and kicked and stamped all the time.

The children watched in astonishment. Then the snow-bird asked if they might have a ride on one of the horses, and the goblins said yes, certainly. So up they jumped, and off went the horse with them, rocking all over the cave. Jim and Mollie loved it.

Then the bird took them to where the dolls' houses were being built by tiny pixies. The pixies lived in them, and Mollie thought it was lovely to see them sitting at the little tables on tiny chairs, peeping out of the windows, and sleeping in the small beds.

'Now hurry up, or we shan't have time to see the Christmas trees growing,' said the snow-bird. 'Jump on my back again. They're not far away.'

He took them to a huge field spread with snow. In it were rows and rows of Christmas trees, some very tiny, some bigger, and some so big that Jim and Mollie had to bend their heads back to see the tops.

'Look at the tiny ones,' said Jim. 'They have got little buds on them. Are the buds going to grow into toys, snow-bird?'

'Yes, they are,' said the snow-bird. 'Look at the next row. They are bigger still.'

The children looked. They went from row to row, and saw the toys getting bigger and bigger as the trees grew in size. At first they were tight little buds. Then they loosened a little, and Jim and Mollie could make out a tiny doll, or a little engine. The next size trees had toys a little bigger, and the largest trees of all were dressed with the biggest, loveliest things you could imagine! Fairy dolls, big books, fine engines, great boxes of soldiers, footballs and all kinds of things hung there!

'Will the little trees grow into big trees like this, with all the toys the right size?' asked Mollie.

'Of course,' said the snow-bird. 'Then people buy them. Look, this tree is bought by someone. It has a label on it. It is to be fetched tomorrow.'

Jim read the label.

FOR JACK BROWN'S PARTY, it said.

'Oh!' cried Mollie. 'Why, that's the party we were

going to tomorrow! To think that this lovely tree is going to be there! Oh, I *wish* we were going!'

Her eyes filled with tears, and the snow-bird was terribly upset.

'Don't, please don't,' he begged. 'Look, you shall have a little Christmas tree seed for your own. Plant it, and it will grow into a good size by next Christmas!'

'And have toys on, too?' asked Mollie.

'Certainly,' said the bird. He pressed something into Mollie's hand. She took it. It was a tiny silver ball, the sort you see on Christmas cakes.

'Thank you,' said Mollie. 'I'll be sure to plant it carefully. What fun to have a Christmas tree of my own, with toys and everything on!'

'Now it's time we went back,' said the snow-bird. 'It's nearly seven o'clock by your time, and your mother will want to put you to bed. Jump up again, my dears.'

Up they climbed, and once more the snow-bird flew back into the darkness, leaving the sun far behind him.

The wind blew hard, and the children held on tightly, afraid of being blown off.

'Pff! Isn't the wind strong!' cried the bird. Then suddenly he gave a terrible cry.

'Oh, whatever is it?' cried Mollie.

'The wind has blown away the kingfisher's feather on my head!' cried the bird. 'The magic's going out of me! I shall soon be nothing but a bird made of snow. Oh, oh, I hope you get home safely before that happens!'

He flew more and more slowly, and it seemed to the frightened children as if he were becoming colder and colder. At last he gave a pant, and fell to earth. The children tumbled off, and rolled on the snowy ground. Then they picked themselves up, and looked round.

'Are we home, or not?' asked Jim. 'I can't see the snow-hut or the snowman, can you, Mollie?'

'No,' said Mollie. 'But look, Jim! Isn't that our summer house? Yes, it is! I can just see the weathercock on the top by the light of the stars. We're at the bottom of the garden. The poor old snow-bird couldn't quite get back to the lawn he started from!'

'He's changed into snow and nothing else,' said Jim. 'What a pity that blue feather got blown away.'

'Children, children, didn't you hear me call?' cried Mother crossly, from the window. 'What are you doing out there in the dark? You know you ought to be inside by the fire! Come in at once!'

Jim and Mollie picked up the cushion and ran indoors. They tried to explain to Mother where they had been, and all about the magic snow-bird, but she was too cross to listen. She just popped them into bed, and left them.

But do you know, in the morning the snow-bird was standing at the *bottom* of the garden, and not in the place where Father and Mother had seen him the day before.

'There you are!' cried Jim. 'That just *proves* we are telling the truth, Mummy. How could he have got down there by himself? That shows he *did* take us last night, and couldn't quite get back to the right place.'

'Don't be silly,' said Mother. 'You moved him yourself when you went out to play in the dark after tea yesterday.'

'Well, anyhow, I've got that Christmas tree seed that the snow-bird gave me,' said Mollie. 'I shall plant it, Mummy, and then you'll soon see we are speaking the truth, for it will grow into a proper Christmas tree, all decorated with lovely toys.'

She ran out and planted it in her own little garden. Nothing has come up yet, because it was only a week ago – but wouldn't you love to see everyone's surprise when it really grows into a beautiful Christmas tree, with a fairy doll at the top, and engines, books, teddy bears and other toys hanging all over it?

Acknowledgements

All efforts have been made to seek necessary permissions. The stories in this publication first appeared in the following publications:

'One Christmas Eve' first appeared in *Sunny Stories*, issue 496, 1950

'All the Way to Santa Claus' first appeared in *Sunny Stories*, issue 395, 1946

'Annabelle's Little Thimble' first appeared in *Sunny Stories for Little Folks*, issue 179, 1933

'A Coat for the Snowman' first appeared in *Enid Blyton's Sunny Stories*, issue 370, 1945

'The Extraordinary Christmas Tree' first appeared in *Enid Blyton's Sunny Stories*, issue 395, 1946

'On His Way Home' first appeared in *Crescendo*, 1950

'The Golden Key' first appeared in *Teacher's World*, issue 1067, 1924

'No Present for Benny' first appeared in *Enid Blyton's Sunny Stories*, issue 343, 1944

'First Walk in December' first appeared in *Enid Blyton's Nature Lover's Book*, published by Evans in 1944

'The Christmas Tree Fairy' first appeared in *Enid Blyton's Sunny Stories*, issue 46, 1937

'The Christmas Bicycle' first appeared in *The Christmas Book*, published by Juvenile Productions in 1956

'A Grand Visitor' was first serialised in *Sunny Stories*, issue 21, 1942

'The Little Carol Singer' first appeared in *Crescendo*, 1948

'The Man Who Wasn't Father Christmas' first appeared in *Enid Blyton's Sunny Stories*, issue 258, 1941

'A Christmas Wish' first appeared as 'The Lost Wishing Cap' in *The Teacher's Treasury* [Vol. 1], The Home

ACKNOWLEDGEMENTS

Library Book Company, 1926

'He Belonged to the Family' first appeared in *Daily Mail Annual for Boys and Girls*, 1950

'A Hole in Her Stocking' first appeared in *Enid Blyton's Sunny Stories*, issue 317, 1943

'Christmas in the Toyshop' first appeared as *Oh! What a Lovely Time*, published by Brockhampton in 1949

'They Didn't Believe in Santa Claus!' first appeared in *Sunny Stories*, issue 472, 1949

'Bobbo's Magic Stocking' first appeared in *Sunny Stories for Little Folks*, issue 35, 1927

'The Pantomime Wolf' first appeared in *Junior Printer's Pie*, 1943

'Little Mrs Millikin' first appeared in *Enid Blyton's Sunny Stories*, issue 257, 1941

'Second Walk in December' first appeared in *Enid Blyton's Nature Lover's Book*, published by Evans in 1944

'The Magic Snowbird' first appeared in *Sunny Stories for Little Folks*, issue 86, 1930

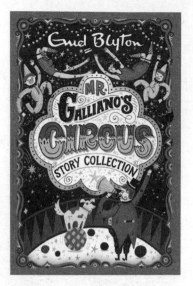

Mr Galliano's Circus

Mr Galliano's famous circus has come to town! Join young Jimmy Brown and his family as they enter a thrilling world of incredible animals, colourful clowns and daring acrobats.

Meet cheeky chimps, kindly elephants, fearsome tigers and one very special little dog called Lucky, as Jimmy discovers what it takes to become part of Mr Galliano's Circus.

This book was previously published as *The Circus Collection*. It comprises three full-length books: *Mr Galliano's Circus*, *Hurrah for the Circus!* and *Circus Days Again*.

Another captivating story collection from Enid Blyton . . .

Brer Rabbit

Brer Rabbit is as clever as can be. He loves to play
jokes and tricks on his animal friends, but every now
and then they get him back!

Join Brer Rabbit, Brer Fox and Brer Bear in over
80 short stories from the UK's favourite storyteller.

Another enchanting story collection from Enid Blyton . . .

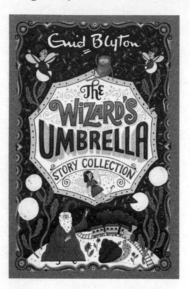

The Wizard's Umbrella

Ribby the Gnome has a very bad habit: he always borrows
things and never brings them back! But when he takes a
wizard's umbrella and doesn't return it, he's in for a horrible
surprise. The umbrella is magic, and it is very angry!

This collection was previously published as
The Chimney Corner Collection.